Executive Action

Executive Action

Jac Simensen

Winchester, UK
Washington, USA

First published by Roundfire Books, 2016
Roundfire Books is an imprint of John Hunt Publishing Ltd., Laurel House, Station Approach,
Alresford, Hants, SO24 9JH, UK
office1@jhpbooks.net
www.johnhuntpublishing.com
www.roundfire-books.com

For distributor details and how to order please visit the 'Ordering' section on our website.

ISBN: 978 1 78535 344 4
Library of Congress Control Number: 2015954382

A CIP catalogue record for this book is available from the British Library.

Design: Stuart Davies

Printed and bound by CPI Group (UK) Ltd, Croydon, CR0 4YY, UK

ONE

The chauffeur pulled the black Lincoln Town Car to the front of a nondescript, office tower in Arlington, Virginia. The building was flanked on either side by identical gray, concrete towers; other than the street numbers above the entrances, the three buildings bore no identification, no company names or logos to suggest what activities might be taking place inside the sterile walls.

The afternoon sky was darkening and the smell of rain or possibly snow hung in the damp air.

A short, wiry man exited from the front passenger seat and opened the rear door for an older man with gold-rimmed glasses and snow-white hair, who unhurriedly swiveled his long legs to the pavement and stepped out of the car.

A third man emerged from the opposite side of the Lincoln; he was broad-shouldered with a thick neck, military-style brush cut, and an obviously muscular body. As he stood, he buttoned his blazer jacket to conceal the semi-automatic pistol that rode in a shoulder holster on his left rib cage. The two other men wore black trench coats over dark business suits with white shirts and conservative neckties.

The broad-shouldered man led the way to the entrance and held the door open for the others. They entered an antiseptic, high-ceilinged lobby where a security guard stood behind a granite counter. On the wall behind the counter hung a four-foot-high metallic sign with the letters *DSC* in blue, against a silver background. At the far end of the lobby were two elevators.

The uniformed guard deferentially nodded to the older man with the white hair. "Afternoon, Doctor Donner."

Doctor Donner smiled. "Tommy, how's your boy, still in Afghanistan?"

"He's stateside now, his mother's thrilled to have him home;

enlistment's up in three more months. Thanks for asking, sir."

"If he's interested, call Jimmy the month before he gets out and we'll find a place for him."

The guard nodded again. "Thank you, sir, I'm sure he'll be very interested in joining DSC." He pushed a button below counter level and an opaque glass panel on the near wall slid open with a soft, pneumatic hiss.

The small man and the muscular man each signed the list of names that lay on the counter, then picked up a badge, and clipped it on their jacket pocket. Doctor Donner didn't bother; it was his company.

The three men walked through the open doorway and into a more comfortable lobby, one with leather furniture, artificial plants, and chrome-framed nature photos on the windowless walls. The opaque glass panel closed behind them. Next to the elevator on the far wall, an attractive, well-dressed woman was seated at a glass and chrome desk.

Doctor Donner removed his overcoat and handed it to the muscular man. "Kurt, have Tilman bring the car around in an hour for the airport." He gestured toward the third man. "Jimmy will be staying here."

Kurt nodded. "Yes, sir. Do I need to call aviation services?"

"Everything's arranged," Jimmy snapped, as he strode to the reception desk.

Doctor Donner turned and followed Jimmy; he extended his hand to the seated woman. "Matty, you're looking especially lovely today. I like the blouse, the pale green goes perfectly with your red hair."

Matty stood, smiled, and took his outstretched hand. Doctor Donner always behaved like a gentleman, but she knew from experience that one comment was his quota for small talk. "Everyone's arrived, Doctor D, they're in the third-floor conference room."

Jimmy had already pressed the call button for the elevator and held the open door.

Doctor Donner nodded to Matty and stepped into the elevator. "You've got the reports?" he asked as the doors closed.

Jimmy handed Donner a black folder sealed in the middle with a strip of silver tape. "Matty distributed the reports to the others when they arrived. I'll destroy the documents when the meeting's finished."

Donner nodded.

Matty picked up the handset from the desktop phone and pushed a button. "Doctor D's on the way," was all she said before replacing the phone in its cradle. For an office receptionist, Matilda Crane had the unusual qualifications of a security clearance and a concealed carry permit for the snub-nosed handgun tucked away in her handbag in a desk drawer.

The third-floor conference room was considerably more opulent than the surrounding Donner Systems Corporation offices. The walls were covered with light-brown padded leather and framed with honey-colored birchwood trim. The oval conference table was of Scandinavian design, in a richly figured birch veneer. The brown, ergonomic leather chairs had been custom designed to match the warm earth tones of the walls, carpet, and furniture and to support the often aching lower backs of the mostly older DSC executives and guests who met in the room. As was the practice before each scheduled meeting, the room had been "swept" that morning for microphones, transmitters, or other intrusive electronics.

Doctor Donner entered, closed the heavy door, and shuffled his six-foot-two frame toward the table. He looked at the three seated men and shook his head. "What a sorry lot of worn-out rogues," he said with a grin.

"Where in hell you been, Nick; we ran out of small talk an hour ago."

Donner extended his hand. "You've been here only six

minutes, Fidel; don't start by trying to make me feel guilty. Remember, I taught you negotiating tactics."

General Thornton grinned, dropped the *Washington Post* he'd been reading, stood, and shook Donner's hand. Major General Frank Thornton, USAF-retired, was a large man with a deep tan and a graying crew cut. He'd been called Fidel for so many years that no one alive could recall how he got the nickname, and Thornton wasn't about to help anyone remember.

Donner beckoned to the small, dark man at the far end of the table. "Avi, come on down to this end where we can see you better, and keep your hands out of your pockets."

Avi laughed. "I'm trying to stay upwind of Jasper; smells like a bloody whorehouse, he does."

Martin Jasper was slim with an angular nose, a receding hairline, and brilliant blue eyes. He was impeccably dressed in a hand-tailored suit, custom-made shirt, and colorful silk tie. Martin rose and shook Donner's hand. "Afternoon, Nicholas," he said in a clipped, British accent. "Can we get right to it? I've a tight schedule."

"Another little boy?" Avi teased as he moved behind Jasper, shook Donner's hand, and slid into the chair on Thornton's right.

Jasper made an obscene hand gesture toward Avi, then swiveled his chair to face Donner.

"Children, children." Donner shook his head while lowering his seventy-four-year-old arthritic body into the leather chair at the head of the table that had obviously been left open for him. He wiped his gold-rimmed glasses with a pocket handkerchief and then broke the silver seal on the black folder with a ballpoint pen. Identical folders sat on the table in front of each man. Following Donner's lead, they broke the seals and examined the pages within in silence.

Five minutes later, General Thornton pushed back in his chair and closed the black folder. "Good news. Looks like they've solved the weight problem; Avi, it's under thirty kilos?"

Avi placed his hands over the folder as if to hide its contents from view. "Assuming the *fruit* comes in at less than eight kilos, they can do it. That's without the shielding, of course; that comes away before the package is deployed."

Doctor Donner swiveled to his right. "Jasper, the fruit?"

"Too early to say; the radiologicals are still being sourced. At the moment, I'd put the probability of achieving eight kilos at ninety percent."

"I'd feel a lot more positive if we could test this thing, lots of untried crap in here," Thornton said, tapping the folder with his index finger.

Donner shook his head. "You know that's impossible, Fidel. Satellites would pick up gamma rays and neutrons no matter what precautions were taken. DSC primed the second-generation Vela Satellites, and the technology's moved several generations beyond Vela since then; radiation from an RDD, even a lightly packed device, would be instantly detected by a dozen satellites."

Avi was perched on the edge of his chair, his arms pulled close against his body like a compact, dark hawk about to take flight. "We're working out a plan for a 'dry' test with tracers instead of the fruit. The real bomb will be considerably dirtier than a conventional radiological dispersal device. The fruit's a multisource cocktail: Strontium-90 surrounded by Cesium-137 and Iodine-131. The iodine kills within days, the other two hang around for decades. The schematics of the antitank shell were the breakthrough we needed to solve the weight problem." He nodded in acknowledgement toward General Thornton. "Give the devil his due."

"Good job, Fidel," Donner added.

Thornton's expression remained unchanged.

Avi continued, "According to the information we have, the antitank shell was tested four times with a small radiological package, but never used in combat. That was in the nineties. The concept's elegant in its simplicity and with today's explosives and electronics it's smaller, lighter, and more deadly. We've tested and retested the electrical and mechanical components without a single unpredicted event—this is gonna work just fine."

"The damage assessment's still the same?" Donner asked.

Avi nodded. "Better; explosion will destroy all non-hardened structures in a radius of a hundred to a hundred-fifty meters; roughly, one hundred yards. The radiation will kill personnel within three hundred meters, with delayed, secondary kill up to half a kilometer."

"And the residual radioactivity?" Thornton asked.

"Depending on the success of their decontamination efforts, the space within two-hundred-fifty meters from the ignition point will be inaccessible for four to five years, possibly longer."

Fidel pointed at Donner. "How about the mule?"

"Early days," Donner replied. "I've got the psychological profiling underway; next meeting I'll have more specifics about the mule."

"You know the mule's the critical link; all this other sophisticated crap won't be worth spit unless we're able to deliver the device to the target."

"Thanks for reminding us of the critical nature of the delivery, Fidel," Donner coolly replied. "Next meeting. Now, unless other salient observations need to be made, let's begin the punch list. Jasper, since you're such a busy fellow, perhaps you could start?"

TWO

"Shannon didn't get no supper, Mrs. Samadi. Her ma's run out of food 'til she gets her card filled up on Saturday."

Mu looked into the third-grader's wide brown eyes. "How do you know that, Ramon; did Shannon tell you?"

"Uh-huh, on the bus this morning she said she was so hungry that her stomach hurt. She asked if I had anything ta eat in my backpack. I only had some gum, but I gave it her. My daddy says that when your empty stomach hurts, that means you're really poor. Daddy says that when he was a kid he was poor but now we're rich."

Mu stroked Ramon's curly, black hair. "Thanks, Ramon; I'll see that Shannon gets somethin' to take home."

"Don't say I told she wouldn't like that much. Shannon's my friend and I don't want her stomach ta hurt."

Mu smiled. "Your secret's safe with me."

"Thanks, Mrs. Samadi."

Mu walked the few steps to the school cafeteria kitchen where a round, black woman wearing a patterned apron was scrubbing a very large pot in the concrete sink. "Shannon Sharp's mom's run out of food-stamp money 'til the weekend," she said. "We'll need another supper bag. You know how many kids in Shannon's family?"

Gladys frowned and nodded. "I surely do. Her mama's a longtime member of our congregation. Jus' little Shannon now; oldest boy got his-self killed in Iraq; got blowed up." Gladys pronounced Iraq as if it were spelled *Eye-Rock*. "Middle daughter got a government job in Tallahassee; then she got herself a fancy boyfriend and don't send money home no more, spends it all in the bars and clubs, so I hear."

"We have much food?"

"There's lotsa white bread, a couple pounds a bologna, and

plenty a peanut butter; more oranges too. Milk's all gone 'til the morning." Gladys lifted the heavy pot onto the drain board. "I got lotsa eggs, but we need those for the kids' breakfast tomorrow."

"How many breakfasts are we making now, Gladys?"

"Officially forty-seven, but then there's always another dozen hungry kids who ain't been signed up yet. I was gonna do French toast with all them eggs an' bread we got, but there's no syrup. Don't think kids would like French toast without the syrup, I know I don't. Think I'll just do scrambled eggs and toast; got lots of ketchup, kids like ketchup on eggs. Sound alright?"

Mu nodded. "That's good—if you make up a few sandwiches for Shannon and her mom that should keep her stomach from hurtin' 'til breakfast; put in some oranges too, okay?"

Gladys sighed loudly. "Feels like we're jes stickin' our fingers in the dike like that kid in the story. Every school year there's more hungry kids to feed. I don't know how much longer I can do this."

Mu wrapped her arms around Gladys's broad girth and kissed her lightly on the cheek. "These are our kids, Gladys, yours and mine. We'll look after 'em like we always have, as long as the Lord allows and the state sends the money."

Gladys returned Mu's embrace and smiled a broad smile that pushed the dimples in her full cheeks up and outward. "You and me, honey, you and me," she whispered in Mu's ear.

Three generations of former Lisson Grove Elementary School students knew Muriel Samadi as the Lunch Lady. Everywhere she went in the community, she was warmly welcomed. "Hey, Mrs. Samadi, what's for lunch?" was a frequent greeting.

Since childhood, Muriel had always been called Mu. Except for Miss Caldwell who taught Home Economics at Baron County High School, everyone called her Mu. Although her performance in the more academic high-school courses was, at best, average, Mu was Miss Caldwell's star pupil. Before she graduated, Miss

Caldwell had Mu baking and decorating fancy cakes, even wedding cakes, on weekends at the Caldwell Family Bakery in town. After graduation, Mu joined the bakery full time, working side by side with Miss Caldwell's elderly father in the early-morning hours, before the bakery opened, learning the baker's fragrant trade.

Mu's post-high-school social life had consisted exclusively of family and church events and occasional birthday parties or wedding showers with her female school friends. She hadn't been asked out on a regular date since eleventh grade. Mu was a big woman. She stood six foot tall, weighed in at about one-sixty-five, and had rather large hands and feet. She had perfect white teeth, a pretty smile, mousey-brown hair that she kept short, and bright brown eyes. Mu's clothing choices leaned toward extreme casual; most of the time she wore tee shirts, sweats, jeans, or knee-length shorts. She wasn't shy, but neither was she particularly outgoing.

When Miss Caldwell's father had a debilitating stroke that ended his life-long love affair with flour, sugar, yeast, and water, Miss Caldwell and Mu tried to keep the bakery afloat, but neither had any experience running a retail operation. When the new Winn-Dixie opened a few miles from the old downtown, the little bakery's fate was sealed.

The thought that she might want to live somewhere other than Lisson Grove never occurred to Mu, so she took the only culinary job in town, replacing the retiring cook at Lisson Grove Elementary. A few years later, Mu moved up to supervisor of the school's food service operation, hired Gladys, and became affectionately and permanently known as the Lunch Lady.

* * *

Rustam Kas Samadi was born and raised in Lisson Grove; no one except his mother ever called him anything but Rusty. Rusty's father was an eccentric who owned the only gas station in town. In his late twenties, Rusty's father had been resettled from Iran to Lisson Grove by the U.S. Government in return for some undefined services he'd provided to one of the U.S. intelligence agencies. Mr. Samadi, Mr. Sam, as the locals promptly named him, chose to remain mysterious, never discussing his Iranian past with his three children or his friends. He was so tight-lipped that Mr. Sam's wife died at age fifty-six without ever learning why she and Ali, her infant son, had been spirited out of Tehran in the middle of the night. Besides Rusty and Ali, the Samadis had a daughter called Shahana.

As they matured, the three Samadi children took turns pumping gas and wiping windshields while Mr. Sam sat at his desk in the cluttered gas-station office that reeked of tobacco, grease, and used motor oil. He chain-smoked Lucky Strikes, while reading volume after never-ending volume of the Great Books of the Western World. He'd been sold the expensive, faux leather, nearly unfathomable set of sixty books on the presumption that reading all of the volumes would provide him with the equivalent of a college education.

Mr. Sam maintained the dream that one day the family would return to Iran, and so he taught both of his boys to speak and read Farsi. Mr. Sam wasn't particularly religious, and since the nearest Islamic Center was more than a hundred miles away, only infrequently did he tutor the boys in Islam and supervise their occasional prayers and readings from the Koran.

One evening a few weeks after Rusty's eighth birthday, a black sedan pulled up at the Samadi home and two men in dark suits knocked on the door. The men and Mr. Sam spent an hour talking in the dining room behind closed doors. The next morning, while the three children waited for the school bus, Ali, with the studied gravitas of the elder brother, told Rusty and Shahana that the family would never return to Iran. That day, the two boys' Farsi lessons and Koran readings came to an abrupt halt.

* * *

Rusty was twenty-three when he met Mu; he liked women and enjoyed sex, but like most things in his life, he didn't go too far out of his way for either. Rusty and Mu first met at Whispering Pines Care Center when Rusty pushed his father's wheelchair into the courtyard flower garden and found Mu sitting on a stone bench reading a food magazine. Rusty's father's Alzheimer's disease had advanced to the stage where he sat soundlessly in his chair with his head down, eyes closed, and mouth agape for all of the hours he wasn't officially sleeping.

Rusty was surprised to find someone in the usually empty atrium and briefly lost control of his father's wheelchair on the ramp that sloped down from the main building, nearly running over Mu's large foot. "Ooops, sorry, that's steeper than I remembered," he apologized.

Mu looked up from her magazine. "No harm done," she said with a smile. "That your father?"

"Yeah, he's got Alzheimer's real bad, can't remember much of anything; doesn't even know his name."

"That's a pity. Didn't he run the Texaco station in town; Mister Sam, right?"

Rusty nodded. "Over twenty years my family owned the garage. I used to work there with my brother."

"You're Shanna Samadi's brother Ali, aren't you? Shanna was in my class."

"I'm Rusty Samadi, Ali's my older brother; I'm two years older than Shanna."

"Right, I remember you from the Texaco station, pumpin' gas. You haven't been around for a while though?"

"I been away, been in the army for three years."

"The army, huh; you got drafted?"

Rusty grinned. "They don't do the draft no more. I joined up right after graduation, didn't know what else to do with myself."

"Get to go anyplace interesting?"

Rusty shrugged. "Not really: Jersey, Virginia; couple other places. Nowhere's I'd hurry back to."

"What'd you do in the army?"

"Fixed trucks and cars, mostly; I'm a mechanic."

Mu set her magazine on the bench and extended her right hand. "I'm Muriel Boyle, everyone calls me Mu."

Rusty bent down and took her hand; Mu smiled as her large hand vanished beneath Rusty's outsized fingers. She looked him over: a tall, muscular young man with dark brown hair and a pleasant, oval-shaped face; probably a few years older and a few inches taller than she. They looked into each other's eyes and held hands for a bit longer than a casual handshake required, until Mu glanced away and placed her hands in her lap. She silently wished she'd worn something more flattering than cut-off jeans, flip-flops, and a tee shirt.

"You visitin' somebody, too?" Rusty asked.

Mu nodded. "My mother; her kidneys are failin', she's on dialysis and fadin' fast."

"That's too bad," Rusty replied. He gestured toward the stone bench opposite the bench where Mu sat. "Mind if I sit down, or maybe you'd rather read?"

"I'm not really interested in the magazine; I just can't stay with my mother for more than a few minutes at a time, she doesn't talk anymore and seldom opens her eyes; watchin' her die makes me really sad."

Rusty swiveled the wheelchair to the side of the path so that his father faced into the garden, and then sat. "I'm surprised I haven't seen you here before, I come see my dad every Saturday and Sunday."

"I usually visit Mama during the week, after work. I get off about three and then stop here on my way home. Been doin' that for the last two months since Mama's been here. My sister and brother-in-law usually come on the weekends. They're movin' to

Colorado; house huntin' now, so I got a cover weekends for 'em."

"You work here in town?"

"Yep, I do, I cook for the kids at the school; used to work at the bakery 'til it shut down."

"The bakery closed? When did that happen?"

"'Bout a year ago."

"Humm," Rusty replied. "Hadn't noticed; I been back from the army about five months. We put my father in here three months ago after we sold the business and our family home. My brother, Ali, and his wife took their share of the money and bought a restaurant in Key West. Shanna had this operation where they tied a string round her stomach so's she can't eat too much; she's gettin' skinny now, you probably wouldn't recognize her; she's a bartender at Ali's place."

"But you still live around here?"

"Uh-huh, used my share of the money to buy a new pickup and a house out on Dorrance Street. Since I got back from the army I been workin' temporary for the county maintainin' their cars and trucks, but I just got a permanent job workin' for the town." He gave her a broad smile. "Nothin' glamorous; drivin' the trash truck. Pays pretty good, with vacations and benefits, and its steady work."

Mu nodded. "Steady's good," she said.

They talked for a while longer and discovered that although Mu was two years younger than Rusty; they had a number of friends and school experiences in common.

Mu was quick to notice that next to Rusty's six-foot-three, muscular, two-hundred-twenty-pound body, her oversize hands and feet didn't look especially large.

When, not by chance, they met in the care-center garden the following Saturday, Rusty was wearing a new black golf shirt, pressed khakis, and polished black shoes. Mu's hair had been styled; she was wearing a sundress that emphasized her full breasts, and she'd applied a touch of lip gloss.

Rusty took Mu to Applebee's for drinks and dinner that evening and then back to his home to watch *Saturday Night Live* on TV. He was surprised to discover that Mu was a virgin, his first, and only. They found that their larger-than-average bodies were ideally matched for exploring the pleasures of the flesh, and their undemanding expectations of life were in perfect synchronization. Mu started spending weekends at Rusty's, and when she found the original Tater abandoned along the road and brought him to live with Rusty, she announced that she needed to move in to care for the kitten. Shortly after, Rusty and Mu married in a civil ceremony at Ali's bar in Key West.

THREE

Rusty and Charley were having a successful day. They'd salvaged an old tiger-maple silverware chest; an antique-looking, child's Windsor chair; a half-dozen elegant, leather-bound books; a bag full of tantalizingly twinkling costume jewelry; a tan Steiff teddy bear with a brass button in its ear and a badly torn, but still attached, right leg; and a paper bag with a dozen or more political campaign buttons from the 1960s and '70s. The passenger seat and floor well of the ancient, creaking trash hauler were nearly full, and they still had one more section of *The Gardens* to collect.

"Whatcha think?" Charley asked, holding up a shallow cardboard box full of sheet music for Rusty's inspection. "Looks old."

"Leo says there's no call for piano music." Rusty extended his well-muscled arms through the truck's window. "Give it here; I'll have a look through at the next stop. Sometimes restaurants like to frame the ones with pictures of famous people: Judy Garland, Sinatra, ones like that."

Charley walked to the rear of the truck, grabbed the handholds, and effortlessly swung up to stand on the rider's platform while Rusty turned the groaning garbage hauler around the corner and onto Paloma Court.

The piano music was commercially uninteresting, mostly religious; Rusty handed the box down to Charley who tossed it into the maw of the gaping loader/compressor at the rear of the truck, dumping coffee grounds and eggshells from the next garbage can on top of the sheet music.

The remainder of their pickups yielded little of value: two small wooden footstools with hand-stitched tapestry covers and a framed photo of a World War II bomber.

When they'd finished the last section of their run, Charley

turned the levers that started the great pneumatic-driven plate on its clamorous journey for the unknown-thousandth time, squeezing, compressing the bi-weekly refuse of a hundred households into a nondescript, reeking mass of plastic garbage bags, wire hangers, cardboard boxes, worn-out shoes—the stinking detritus of South Florida retirement living.

Charley threaded his lanky frame onto the well-worn passenger's seat, twisting his legs around their newly acquired treasures and, with some difficulty, pulled the door shut.

As Rusty shifted into first gear, Charley closed one eye and curled his lips. "Them books should get at least ten apiece, and the box thirty." He counted on his fingers. "When Leo gets the bear sewed up it'll probably get fifty. The buttons and jewels gotta be another twenty; lots more if any of that stuff's silver or gold or got real stones. Don't know about them stools and that chair." He looked down at his fingers. "Two hundred, maybe two-ten; sixty, seventy for each of us, that's good."

Rusty grunted. "Real good, better'n we done in a while."

"Like you said, when the snowbirds go home they always throw out good stuff."

"Always," Rusty replied. "I figure some of them save stuff to pack in the car for their kids, then the car's too full or they decide that the kids won't want the stuff, and chuck it out instead. Easter's late this year, so we'll probably be gettin' more good stuff for another three, four weeks, 'til they're all gone back north."

Charley shifted in his cramped seat, moving the child's chair from the foot well onto his lap. "You gonna stop at Leo's or go straight to the dump?"

"I'd rather not stop, don't want Leo's neighbors complainin' 'bout the stink. Depends whether you can make it to the pickup without gettin' cramped up?"

"Yeah, I can make it; this isn't bad, not like that elephant foot we got last year."

Rusty grinned. "Yeah, the umbrella stand; that sucker was

really big."

"Stunk, too; almost made me heave," Charley replied. "Worth it though. Leo got three hundred for the thing."

"Never ceases to amaze me how you remember numbers, I think you could tell me the price of every piece of crap we sold over the last five years."

"Probably could. Doctors say that's account of where the bullet went in my head: screwed up all the wires for remem-berin' what I'm 'posed to remember and pushed the wires into the part of my brain that does the numbers. Wanna know the plate numbers of the cars we passed this morning? I can remember 'em all."

"I know you can; I don't need another demo to believe you. Ya know we should get you on TV, one of them reality shows, people would be amazed."

Charley frowned. "Don't want anyone to know where I am; don't wanna go on the TV."

Rusty sensed Charley's agitation and quickly changed the subject. "What ya say we drop the stuff at the pickup first, then we'll dump the load and take the stuff to Leo's? We can clean up there and then go on down to Brownie's for lunch. Whatcha say?"

Charley smiled. "I like the fish sandwiches at Brownie's; he does good fish—"

"No pineapple juice; you don't wanna puke up the fish like last time," Rusty interrupted.

"I don't drink pineapple juice no more."

Rusty prodded him. "Just makin' sure you remember."

Six years ago Rusty Samadi had agreed to take on Charley Hocter as his helper on a trial basis; they'd been coworkers and friends ever since. In his former life, Charley had been a Marine Corps platoon leader and then a successful loan officer at an S & L in Fort Myers. During an attempted heist, the nervous, first-time bank robber's hand shook so badly that he accidentally pulled the trigger, sending a bullet careening off the panicked teller's marble countertop, through a glass door panel, and into Charley's head.

Charley survived, and after six weeks and two operations, he was moved from a hospital to a rehabilitation center.

Charley's lawyer took a large bite of the settlement he extracted from the bank's insurance company; the hospital and doctors took an even bigger share; and then, unbeknownst to Charley, his wife sold their house and possessions, emptied their joint bank account, and moved to Hawaii with her new boyfriend, an orderly she'd met while visiting Charley at the hospital.

Charley's prognosis for recovery from extensive brain damage was mixed. He could see, hear, and speak normally, but he'd lost the ability to read more than simple sentences and couldn't write at all. He'd also traded his command of words for advanced number-manipulation skills, leaving him with the vocabulary of a child. His coordination and motor skills seemed unimpaired, but his memory, like his brain, had some serious holes. He knew that he had had a wife and recognized her photos, but confused her with his sister and was convinced that she had died from breast cancer years before. When the rehabilitation center's social worker discovered that other than his wife, Charley had no living relatives, she decided there would be nothing to gain from telling him about Hawaii or the boyfriend, and so, Charley's wife remained deceased.

Charley's post-surgery mental capabilities were evaluated and he was classified as "Trainable." The psychologist explained that Charley didn't have the intellectual capacity to hold down more than a menial job, but with continuous oversight he would most likely be able to live on his own.

When his remaining money ran low, the rehabilitation center contacted the Veteran's Administration, and eventually Charley was placed in a VA foster-care program in Lisson Grove.

He and Bert, an older navy vet with one arm, lived in Mrs. Jeannie Kovacs' home. Each of the men had their own room and bath; they shared a lounge with a TV and a phone. They got along well; Bert talked a lot and Charley was good at listening.

Mrs. Kovacs was a widow and kept her home spotlessly clean. Under the occasional supervision of a VA dietitian, she cooked two nutritious meals each day, and she and the two men ate dinner together as a family.

After bingo one Thursday, Mrs. Kovacs told Father Jerry about Charley and Father Jerry asked about Charley's religious affiliation. Next day, she asked Charley if he had been brought up Catholic. Charley didn't know what a Catholic was but thought that he might offend Mrs. Kovacs if he said otherwise, so he said "sure."

When Father Jerry visited Mrs. Kovacs' house to meet with Charley, Bert went to his room; he said he was a Baptist and didn't want anything to do with Catholic priests.

The next weekend, Mrs. Kovacs took Charley with her to Saturday confession and to Sunday mass, she was pleased to have his company. He quickly caught on to the routine of the mass but had a hard time with confession and sin. Charley couldn't comprehend why he needed to tell Father Jerry about bad things he'd done; after all, he wanted Father Jerry to like him and be his friend. At home, he and Mrs. Kovacs talked about sin, and Mrs. Kovacs gave Charley examples of the kinds of sins people would confess. Charley settled on two: taking the Lord's name in vain, and thinking impure thoughts. Every Saturday afternoon thereafter he piously confessed to both, said his Hail Marys and Our Fathers, and went home with a smile on his face and peace in his heart.

* * *

Rusty honked the horn twice and pulled the red Ford F-150 up to the side door of the barn. A flock of chickens noisily scattered as the truck approached. A slim, brown-skinned woman dressed in plaid shorts and a tee shirt lettered in Spanish emerged from the modest, concrete-block house onto the screened back porch and waved. "Leo's not here," she hollered. "He's at the shop, said he'd be back about five."

Rusty climbed down from the driver's seat while Charley came around and dropped the pickup's tailgate. "Hey ya, Rosa," Rusty replied. "Just gonna leave some stuff we picked up today and then wash up."

Charley waved with both hands. "Goin' ta Brownies for fish," he called out with a smile.

Rosa's jet-black hair hung in a single braid down the middle of her back. "Come in for lemonade when you're finished. Leo left an envelope for you."

"We're goin' ta Brownie's," Charley repeated.

"Be there in ten," Rusty called out to Rosa. "Then we'll go to Brownie's," he said to Charley.

Charley nodded and began to unload their new finds from the bed of the truck. Rosa went back into the house.

Rusty grasped the bunch of keys that were dangling on a silver spring-loaded key chain attached to his belt. He found the key he wanted, unlocked and removed the brass padlock and opened the heavy, steel-reinforced door, then turned on the interior lights.

Charley carried the child's chair and the stack of books inside and set them on a large plywood sheet that rested on metal sawhorses just inside the door. "Jesus H. Christ, it stinks in here," he said unemotionally. Charley rarely swore, but he made sure to get in a few blasphemies each week before his Saturday confession.

Rusty pointed toward the roof. "It's all them books up in the loft; Leo never finished clearin' 'em out after '*Dolly*.' They're full a mold and not good for nothin' cept startin' fires. You know Leo; can't get rid of anything that might be worth a dime." The 'Dolly' Rusty referred to was a Category-4 hurricane that had roared through Baron County, leaving millions of dollars of havoc and Leo's sodden books in its wake.

Leopold Zornig was a trader and a pack rat who lived by his wits. Leo ran a pawnshop off Route 19 on the outskirts of the town of Lisson Grove in Baron County. Besides the pawnshop, Leo owned an antiques business that was nestled among a dozen or so antique and collectable shops, ice-cream parlors, tearooms, and luncheonettes along a three-block section of restored 1930s and '40s buildings that fronted the dusty main street of Lisson Grove. The town was part of an inland farming community with orange groves, cattle, and more recently a huge warehouse and distribution center just east of the interstate. Although most of the "antiques" for sale in Lisson Grove's shops were of the country decorator style and not particularly valuable, downtown Lisson Grove drew a steady mix of locals, winter residents, day trippers, and tourists.

After the day's treasures were safely in the barn, Rusty locked the door and he and Charley walked to the opposite side of the house where a large porcelain wash basin had been set up on cinderblocks. Charley stripped out of his signal-orange, town-supplied coveralls to his clean tee shirt and shorts. Rusty took off his white, sleeveless undershirt and used the bar of brown laundry soap to wash his hands and arms, rinsing the residue off with the hose that hung coiled next to the washbasin.

While Charley washed up, Rusty went into the screened porch and knocked on the open kitchen door.

Rosa was stirring the contents of a big pot atop the black, eight-burner gas stove Leo had salvaged from a restaurant. "Come on in, Rusty." She turned her head toward him. The wrinkles from five children and a lifetime of challenges were etched into her face, yet it was still a pleasant face, an optimistic face. "You want some lemonade? Glasses are on the counter and pitcher's in the fridge. Be with you in a minute."

"Thanks, Rosa. I better pass on the lemonade; Charley's anxious to get ta Brownie's, got his heart set on a grouper sandwich. You know how antsy he gets when what's left of his mind gets focused on somethin'."

Rosa tapped the wooden stirring spoon on the rim of the large pot and placed the bowl of the spoon in a saucer next to the stove. She turned toward Rusty and the open door. "Poor Charley," she said, shaking her head sympathetically. "Wanna take some of this chili home to Mu? I made a whole lot; Four and his girlfriend are coming over for dinner."

Rusty grinned. "I forget; which one's Four?"

"Joaquin," Rosa replied. "He's the only one Leo still calls by his nickname; he's got me doin' it now. Joaquin doesn't mind, in fact, his girlfriend calls him Four. Maria-Rosa was the only one of the kids who seriously objected to being called a number, even though she was number One. She's in Panama with her husband; hasn't been home in two years. Joaquin and Ernesto are the two I see regularly, the other two got jobs in California. Ernesto's an assistant chef at a big hotel in Naples; Leo's very proud of him. Don't ever say nothin', but Ernesto's always been Leo's favorite. He was the only one of the five children who was still a baby when we moved in with Leo. I'm sure Leo thinks of Ernesto as his natural son, and Ernesto's never known a father other than Leo—Here I go blubbering on and I know you gotta get moving. The envelope's on the table under the saltshaker. Let me get a container for the chili." She rummaged in the white kitchen cabinet below the counter and found a plastic container with a snap-on lid, then filled it with simmering chili. "This is hot stuff. I'll put it in a bag you can carry by the handles. Tell Mu not to bother returnin' the container. It came from the market with potato salad. I don't need it back."

"Smells spicy," Rusty said. "Mu's gonna like this a lot. Thanks,

Rosa."

Rusty carefully placed the brown paper bag into the silver tool chest that was welded to the pickup's bed and then raised the tailgate. He waved to Rosa and opened the truck door; Charley sat staring forward, drumming his fingers on his knees.

Rusty started the truck and shifted into reverse. "Okay, Charley, one grouper sandwich comin' up."

Charley smiled.

* * *

"Tater!" Rusty called from the back door. "Tater, come get your supper."

A large black cat stuck his head out of the palmetto brush to the rear of the house. "Here ya are," Rusty called out as he put a white plastic bowl on the concrete porch. Rusty yawned; he'd been up since four. He waited as the cat languidly made his way to the porch, and then he scratched Tater behind the ears and rubbed under his chin. "Your mother be home in a few hours; time for our nap."

Tater-Two was busily eating his supper but paused momentarily to look up at Rusty and yawn.

Rusty returned to the kitchen and took the canary-yellow notepad from beside the telephone. *Hey, Babe,* he printed, *got some nice stuff this morning and there's forty-five more for the kids. Rosa sent you some chili, I put it in the fridge; she said to keep the container. The mail's on the table; there's a special letter for you! See you at 6. . . . Love, R.*

During most of the school year, Rusty and Mu's work schedules conflicted. Rusty rose at four in the morning, picked up Charley at Mrs. Kovacs house at four-forty and then started their garbage collection rounds at five. Most days, they'd finish between twelve-thirty and one. After Rusty checked the ancient garbage hauler's oil and hydraulic fluids and hosed down the outside of the truck, he and Charley would go into town for lunch. Usually, Rusty would drop Charley off and be home by two when he'd feed the cat and nap until six.

Mu got up at six, after Rusty had gone, and was at the nearby school by six-forty-five. She'd help serve breakfast and lunch, coordinate the planning and provision of deliveries for the next day's meals, and then leave for home at three. On Tuesdays and Thursdays she'd shop for groceries at the new Winn-Dixie, or drive the fourteen miles to the Walmart Super Center if she or Rusty needed clothing, personal items, or a prescription refill. On Mondays, Wednesdays, and Fridays, Mu would prepare a special dinner, shower, and then, at six, slide her naked body into bed beside Rusty. After she creatively woke him and began foreplay, they would energetically make love until both of them were satisfied and ready for dinner.

Tater had made his way in through the cat door and was bathing himself on the bed, lying in a spot of late-afternoon sun. "Be right there, you lazy good for nothing." Rusty called to the cat as he finished shaving and wiped the remaining foam from his face. It was Wednesday and Rusty needed to be washed and clean-shaven to please Mu.

FOUR

There were only four passengers in first class and, of the more than two hundred coach seats, only seventy were filled. Not counting the Conviasa Airlines Airbus 340's cargo hold, the weekly, round-trip flight from Caracas to Damascus, continuing on to Tehran, was always lightly loaded. Reservations for the flight, in either direction, could be placed only through an unlisted phone number that connected to an apartment somewhere in Venezuela. Anyone attempting to make a reservation for this flight through the normal, commercial Conviasa booking system would be politely told that no such flight existed.

Martin Jasper was seated on the aisle in the front row of first class. He was on the return flight from Damascus to Caracas and was reading a copy of the Syrian newspaper *Al-Thawra* published in Arabic. The seat beside him and the two across the aisle were unoccupied. Martin Jasper was nearly always addressed by his surname alone, just Jasper. He was a man with few friends, Nicholas Donner being a member of that small group.

Jasper had first met Doctor Donner twenty years ago; they'd been introduced by a senior officer at the National Security Agency, the U.S. agency responsible for eavesdropping—collecting and interpreting foreign intelligence and protecting U.S. Government and Military communications. Donner's company, Donner Systems Corporation, was a frequent contractor or subcontractor to NSA, and, at that time, was involved in the design and implementation of a voice communications surveillance-monitoring network. NSA and DSC were both experiencing difficulty securing the cooperation of a critical partner, a British telecommunications company, for a Middle Eastern node in the network and were looking to Jasper for help.

Jasper's family on his father's side was descended from an Irish baronet, and his mother's forbearers were long-standing members of the English officer corps, with generals and brigadiers among them. Jasper's grandfather had served with T. E. Lawrence, aka Lawrence of Arabia, and as a young boy Jasper basked in his grandfather's frequent retelling of his adventures in Egypt and the Arabian Desert. He read and reread Lawrence's *Revolt in the Desert* and decided to follow in Lawrence's footsteps. He took a degree in archaeology at Oxford, where he threw himself into his studies at the expense of a student social life, and, like Lawrence, became fluent in multiple languages, including Arabic, Farsi, and Syriac. While at university, he joined expeditions to Petra in Jordan and other ancient Middle Eastern sites in Syria and Lebanon. In Syria, Jasper studied Islam and briefly toyed with the prospect of converting but, in the end, decided that Islam's restrictions on alcohol weren't worth assuming in exchange for the uncertain prospect of an afterlife of heavenly bliss.

After graduation, Jasper accepted a position with the British Museum as a liaison officer to the government of Syria, based in Damascus. Then, suddenly, at age thirty, Jasper lost all interest in the ancient world and its treasures when his latent homosexuality erupted in an emotional torrent unleashed by a beautiful, doelike, French-Syrian boy of nineteen called Jimal. For the first time in his life, Jasper was hopelessly, foolishly in love. He doted on Jimal, bringing thick, strong coffee to his bed each morning, continually buying expensive presents for him in the souk, and exploring the acts of forbidden love in the dark.

Within a month of becoming aware of his sexual orientation, Jasper's first taste of romantic passion was shattered when he discovered that Jimal, his exquisite lover, was a prostitute; a prostitute with another lover, a German heavy-equipment salesman. Jasper found them together in his apartment one afternoon, the delicate Jimal and the great Teutonic hairy-ape.

Jasper was devastated; he was angry, jealous, hurt, betrayed, frightened, and embarrassed. He resigned his position and returned to London to drink excessively, socialize nonstop, and explore his newfound bisexuality.

Eventually, a bisexual university friend arranged an interview for him with Government Communications Headquarters, GCHQ, the British equivalent of the American NSA. His language skills and Middle Eastern familiarity fit GCHQ needs and Jasper got the job, soldiering on for the next five years doing top-secret but progressively uninteresting translation.

When Jasper's unmarried elder brother was killed in a hunting accident, Jasper inherited the family title, Baronet of Muir. The title, although outside of the peerage, came with some property that produced a modest income. Jasper promptly resigned from GCHQ and rented an apartment in Damascus; he spent the next two years of his life shuttling between parties and social events in London and Damascus.

In Damascus, a former intelligence colleague asked Jasper to take on a low-level surveillance assignment; Jasper agreed, enjoyed the work, and began to fashion a lucrative career for himself. From his British Intelligence Community contacts, his family's old-boy network, his language skills, and his Middle Eastern contacts, not to mention the prestige and barely sustaining income of a Hereditary Baronet, Sir Martin Jasper wove a web of profitable mystery. He became a go-between, a deal facilitator, an introduction maker, and a payment conduit between East and West. It was financially rewarding but potentially dangerous work. Jasper lived by only two rules: rule one, never get caught by his Western customers in an activity they would consider traitorous; and rule two, never give his Middle Eastern customers reason to kill him. Jasper knew that his current project would violate both rules.

Jasper had a three-day-old beard and was dressed in fashionably worn-in designer jeans with a brown cotton sweater over a tan silk turtleneck. He'd removed his expensive, handmade, ankle-high boots; shoved them under the seat; and was settled in for the long, monotonous flight to Caracas. As was his policy, he'd refrain from alcoholic beverages until he arrived at his London flat and retrieved a bottle of fine French or Italian wine from his small but excellent wine cellar.

A squat, dark-skinned man with curly, black hair who was dressed in a tan business suit and a yellow shirt buttoned at the neck, but without a tie, passed along the aisle and entered the toilet in first class at the front of the plane. When Jasper had boarded the aircraft, he'd noticed the man seated three rows behind, and when Jasper placed his carry-on into the bin above his seat, he and the man furtively exchanged glances without signaling any trace of recognition. Jasper knew the man; he was a Hezbollah operative, one he had briefly met in Lebanon only a few months earlier.

Jasper heard the toilet flush; shortly after, without glancing in Jasper's direction, the man returned to his seat, unobtrusively dropping a magazine onto the empty seat across the aisle from Jasper as he passed. Jasper waited five minutes before he stood, placed the Syrian newspaper he'd finished reading over the magazine on the opposite seat, and then walked the few steps to the forward toilet. When Jasper returned he retrieved his Syrian newspaper and the magazine beneath. Before he sat, he looked back several rows toward the man in the light-brown suit; the man's seat was reclined and he was pushed back with his eyes closed.

Jasper casually thumbed through the Iranian Farsi magazine until he found a page with a dog-eared lower corner. He scanned the story on the page until he found a paragraph that discussed the quality differences between Russian- and German-made machine tools. The corners of his full lips rose in a taut smile and he relaxed; the magazine was his receipt for the lethal items he'd purchased in Iran, items he now knew rode in the cargo hold below.

After the flight landed in Caracas, Jasper would leave a coded message for General Thornton that the *fruit* had arrived. Jasper was booked on a late-morning flight from Caracas to Miami and would spend the night there at an airport Holiday Inn Express before catching a Virgin Atlantic flight home to London. He'd almost finished his part, now it was up to the General to manage the transport of the two, shielded containers from Caracas airport to Avi Tesla's Tri-Gen Corporation.

FIVE

"Ricky, Father's acting really strange. I talked with Sally last night and she said that he's hanging out with Fidel. You know Fidel is big trouble."

"Has he gone off his meds?" Rick asked.

"I don't know anything about meds."

"Yes, you do, Cyn. Remember when Nick bankrolled that coup attempt in Central America? That happened when he stopped taking his pills. Fidel was in on that too, if I'm not mistaken."

"I don't remember, Ricky. I don't think he takes pills anymore. That was years ago, before Sally; Sally's done a good job of keeping him out of trouble, but I think she's too wrapped up in her work now to pay attention to Father. She said rumors of a Nobel Prize are circulating."

"Ha!" Rick grunted so loudly that Cynthia had to move the phone away from her ear. "Sally's a smart cookie, but her research isn't Nobel material. Maybe she's been taking his meds."

Cyn sighed. "You're right; Sally's been acting strange for the last couple years. She's started talking to herself like all the other MIT weirdos."

"Besides hanging with Fidel, what's Nick been doing that's got you worried?"

"I was at the house this past weekend and Baynard Fulton called looking for Father. You remember Baynard?"

"Help me," Rick asked. "He's that pompous old fart from the yacht club, the one with all the hair and the Victorian-looking beard and sideburns; the banker, right?"

"He's bald and doesn't have a beard anymore, but yeah, that's Baynard. Baynard said there was a regatta committee meeting Saturday, and Father didn't show and never called. Not like Father, he said; hasn't blown off a committee meeting in twenty years, wanted to know if he was in the hospital."

"That is strange; other than Donner Systems, the New York Yacht Club's the only thing Nick's ever really cared about—and you and Taylor, of course."

"You got it right the first time," she said.

"What do you want me to do, Cyn?"

"Could you call Taylor? Ask him to nose around the company and see if there's anything unusual going on with Father. Taylor thinks I'm a flake, but he'll listen to you. Would you mind terribly?"

"I don't understand. Specifically, what do I ask Taylor?"

Cyn pushed her long auburn hair away from the phone and exhaled through her nose. "See if Father's set up any task forces lately, task forces reporting to him. Money too; look for unallocated pools of money, probably funds under Father's control for unspecified R&D. That's how he usually does it."

"Does what?" Rick asked.

"You know, whatever it is he and Fidel are planning; buying a country, bankrolling a revolution, assassinating the Arch-Duke of Austria."

Rick frowned. "You know I always wind up with a bloody nose when I get involved with your father."

Cyn started to protest.

"Hang on," he said. "I have a lunch meeting with your brother and his guys, on Thursday; Donner Systems is still my most important client. I'll get Taylor aside after the meeting and tell him about your concerns, okay?"

"Thanks, Ricky, thanks so much." She realized that she was unconsciously playing with her wedding ring, twisting it around on her finger. "Have you thought about coming up to the flat this weekend; it's been two weeks. You have plans?"

Rick paused, dramatically. "Only Saturday night, I'm going to a party, orgy actually, couple of George Mason co-eds; other than that, not a thing."

Cyn laughed. "Afraid your frat-house orgy days are long behind you, Casanova. Why don't you catch the train up and we'll see what we can put together on our own. I'll be in the city on Friday at the MET. I could pick up some groceries and cook, or we could go to *The Bucket*?" The Bucket was their private name for whatever local restaurant they currently and regularly frequented. They'd found their first Bucket on their honeymoon, a local no-name bar near a ski resort in Stowe that, on the second visit, they christened The Bucket of Blood. Their current New York City Bucket was Carmine's Italian at the Seaport.

Rick cleared his throat. "Don't know, Cyn; been traveling, I'm really beat. I need a relaxing weekend; hang out, read the papers, watch a horror movie, stuff like that."

"It'll be relaxed, I promise; no histrionics or arguments. Two loving days, just like old times; we'll go for a walk in the rain, I'll order rain."

"Don't know, Cyn," he said.

"There's someone?"

"Nobody except the girls from George Mason," he laughingly replied. "Like we agreed, you'll be the first to know. And you?"

"Nobody—come on up, you won't regret it; I need to be with you, it's important. We need to talk about some things."

"What things?"

"Happy things; no arguments, I swear." She crossed her heart.

Rick paused for several seconds. "Okay, I'll call when I get in the city; should be at the flat by seven. Would you mind cooking? Your garlic shrimp and linguine with a Caesar would be perfect; I'll pick up a baguette from the French bakery in the terminal. As I recall there's at least a case of decent wine left in the cooler. And, can you hold the rain 'til Sunday afternoon?"

"Ooooh, I'm so happy!" she gushed. "We'll have a perfect, relaxing weekend, just like old times."

"Like old, old times, I hope?"

"Like when we were sophomores. See you Friday night; love

ya, night, night."

Rick turned off his cell phone and slowly shook his head.

* * *

Taylor Donner was straight out of central casting; the picture of a successful Washington insider. His conservative, obviously custom-tailored, dark-blue suit with the required American-flag lapel pin was complemented by a yellow silk Countess Mara necktie and a crisp white shirt adorned with Air-Force-One souvenir cufflinks bearing the Presidential seal. His perfectly styled dark-brown hair was beginning to gray around the temples, lending his lean, six-foot frame an air of gravitas befitting the president and CEO of a major supplier of technology to the United States Government intelligence and defense communities.

At fifty-four, Rick Cappa was a slightly older, five-foot-ten version of Taylor Donner; same uniform, minus the Presidential cufflinks.

While the Latino busboys cleared the debris from the four departed diners, Rick moved around the circular table in the private dining room to sit next to Taylor. The two men were drinking espresso; Taylor smoking the one Jamaican cigar he allowed himself each day.

"I'm sure you noticed that Carstairs is coming along well," Taylor said. "His relationships at TSA have been helpful in positioning us in the proposals Solient are priming. Thanks for recommending him."

"Never know how these senior military types will work out. Seems to be binary, they're either exceptional at real world relationships or they flame out completely."

Taylor nodded. "Pier-Carlo called yesterday afternoon; his usual sly, sophisticated, overly friendly self. Seems I owe you another one, he never mentioned Dunbarton. We spent nearly an hour going over current opportunities; looks like our relationship's been restored to where it was two months ago, before the blowup. . . You met with him recently I gather?"

"We had lunch in Milan last Thursday, before the opera."

"La Scala?"

Rick grinned. "He wanted to give me a ride in his new Ferrari, drove it over from the factory the day before; one incredible, gorgeous, machine. Speaking of gorgeous, he had his mistress join us for lunch; Pola, you've met her?"

"He spares me the embarrassment, probably because Gilly's friendly with his wife."

Rick finished his coffee and placed his napkin on the table. "I'm glad he called. You never know if Pier-Carlo will really carry through on his promises."

Taylor pushed his chair back from the table. "Rick, I need to get going. What was it that you wanted to discuss?"

"Cynthia," Rick said flatly. "She thinks that your father may be getting into something crazy again. He's been hanging around with the General, she said."

Taylor frowned. "Fidel?"

"Yep; Sally told her that Fidel calls often, and came to the house for a visit while Sally was at work, maid told her. I know Thornton's on the DSC Board, could have been company business."

"Don't think so," Taylor said, shaking his head. "Unlike most company boards, DSC's is largely ceremonial, it's a place for Father, as chairman, to hold court with his old pals; real work gets done in the committees."

"There's more—Cyn said Nick blew off a regatta meeting at the Yacht Club; never called them. Baynard Fulton phoned to see if Nick had died."

Taylor groaned. "Baynard Fulton, now there's a name from the past. Never could stand the guy."

"That makes two of us; three, counting Cyn."

"That is serious. For Father, New York Yacht Club meetings are like audiences with the Pope. Okay, I'll have my guys check on activities in the chairman's office. Tell Cynthia I'll get back to her; better still, I'll call you and you can translate for my little sister. You're still my brother-in-law, aren't you? I mean legally?"

Rick drummed his fingers on the linen tablecloth. "You know Cyn and I are legally separated; we split our assets down the middle. Cyn kept her Beacon Hill town house, of course, and I took the Watergate condo, but we still jointly own the flat on Saint James in TriBeCa. If you were asking if she kept all of her DSC stock, she did; that's got nothing to do with me."

"I wasn't asking about the stock and I didn't mean to pry," Taylor apologized. "It's just that I get confused by the two of you; Cynthia talks about your marriage like nothing's changed, and I don't see you playing the footloose bachelor with the attractive, obviously available women in this glass cage we live and work in."

Rick lowered his head to his chest and took a deep breath. He looked up and stared intently into Taylor's eyes. "You're probably the only other person on earth who could comprehend what's going on between Cyn and me. I love Cyn, no matter what happens I'll always love her. There's no doubt in my mind that she feels the same way about me. The thing is we can't live together anymore. Two, three days are great, but then, day by day, we slowly find creative methods to torture each other. She gets hyperemotional, I pretend to ignore her; she argues, I sulk and go for long walks; she becomes miserable, I get more miserable than her, but try not to show it. We've tried counseling; I'm sure she needs some serious, psychological attention, more than what that quack therapist she swears by can provide, but she refuses to see a real doctor. Nothing's worked, we've both been unhappy for a long time, that's why we separated. Cyn's work at the museum consumes her and mine keeps me as busy as I allow. We meet in the flat sometimes and live like nothing's changed. She's deliriously happy, like when we first met. We make love a lot, we go for walks. I take her clothes shopping for pretty, provocative, sexy things. She never ages, you know; no wrinkles or gray hair, hasn't put on a pound in the last thirty years. We go out to dinner, once in a while a show or concert. No friends, ever; just the two of us alone. I'm full up and thoroughly content. Then an alarm goes off; something she's said or implied, something I've said that I can see from her expression has hurt her—I know it's time to go."

"How often does this happen, I mean, you two meeting in your apartment?"

"Started right after the separation; it was just six weeks after when she called. We spent a long weekend. Then we started meeting once a month. Now it's twice a month, I'm going up on Friday."

"She's always the one who calls?" Taylor asked.

Rick nodded. "That's been our pattern. Lately, I've been acting like a pimply adolescent waiting for a girl to respond to an offer for a prom date. I sit around on pins and needles during the week waiting for her call and, at the same time, dreading the prospect of our meeting and parting. I've decided to tell her that we've gotta stop seeing each other. I'm starting to shrivel up inside, shrivel up emotionally just like a prune. I'm not sure how I feel about much of anything lately. Why don't you call me next week and ask me your question then; ask me if I'm still your brother-in-law, officially."

Taylor stood and offered his hand. "No matter what you two decide, know that I'd be devastated without your counsel. I think of you as an extension of myself, the better part of my business judgment. You know that I trust you implicitly. Brother-in-law or not, that won't change."

Rick grasped Taylor's hand in a nontraditional handshake. "Thanks, Taylor; I'm really touched, really. You can always count on me being in your corner."

Taylor laughed. "My cut man?"

"The way you've been getting punched around by Appropriations lately, a cut man is what you need. I'm meeting with Senator Toomey Wednesday. Anything I should tell him?"

"Whatever you need to, whatever he wants to hear." Taylor strode toward the exit. "And tell Cyn I'll check on the old man," he called over his shoulder.

SIX

Rick was about to slip his key into the lock when the apartment door unexpectedly opened. Cynthia Donner stood in the doorway, her trim figure silhouetted by the light from the setting sun pouring in through the floor-to-ceiling windows behind. Cyn was wearing a dazzling smile and a diamond necklace, a present Rick had given her for her forty-fifth birthday, and nothing else.

Rick grinned from ear to ear and slowly shook his head. "And what if I was the *Super*, finally come up to fix that dripping toilet?"

"Roscoe called from the lobby, I knew it was you," she purred.

"Evening, Cynthia, Ricky," Mrs. Katz said nonchalantly, as she stepped out from the door across the hallway. Cha-Cha, Mrs. Katz' aged Pomeranian strained on her lead to sniff Rick's shoes. "Is it a private party or can anyone join in?"

"Sorry, Ethel, strictly private tonight," Cyn said, as she grasped Rick's necktie and gently pulled him through the door.

"Rats!" Mrs. Katz called, as the door closed.

Cyn slipped her arms under Rick's suit jacket and pressed her naked body against him, and, in the process, broke the baguette Rick held in his left hand. He dropped the baguette and his leather briefcase to the floor and wrapped his hands around her rear.

"Can't wait any longer," she murmured breathlessly as she tore at his belt.

The trail of men's clothing led from the entry hall to the king-sized bed: a jacket, two shoes and socks, trousers, a shirt, and underwear.

Cyn slipped her hand under the sheet. "I think you're wrong," she cooed, with a mischievous grin. "He's not tired at all; he wants to come out and play."

Rick firmly grasped her wrist through the covers, "Later, Cyn, at bedtime; give it a rest for now."

She withdrew her hand and rolled from her side to her back. "I wish I smoked," she pouted. "I get anything I want; toys too?"

Rick pushed his body up and kissed her nose. "Trapeze, pogo stick, whatever I'm physically capable of doing before my coronary, I promise."

She grinned. "What time do you wanna go to bed then?"

* * *

Rick took the bottle of Chablis from the wine cooler, returned to the walnut and leather barstool, and pulled up to the granite-topped island that separated the great room from the kitchen. He opened the bottle and half filled their glasses. "You were right about your father; Taylor called while I was on the train. Not a lot of detail, but Taylor's sure that Nick's up to something, something he wants kept secret."

"I knew it!" she exclaimed.

"He and Fidel have been meeting with a number of unsavory characters over the last year or so, meeting on a regular schedule: ex-Mossad agents, spy types, arms dealers. Nick's been using the company jets to travel out of the country pretty often. He's paying for everything except the jets with his own funds, so Taylor can't tell about the scale of whatever it is he's up to. He said we'd talk next week."

"How did Tay find out so quickly?"

"He didn't say, but from our brief conversation, I got the distinct impression that Taylor's got an insider, someone on Nick's staff."

"Not likely," she said. "Jimmy's been with Father since forever, since he left the navy, and Kurt would step in front of Father to take a bullet, if necessary, I'm positive he would. Other than those two, everyone who works with Father are regular DSC employees, people who come and go depending on the projects Father's working on. Not likely there's an insider."

Rick shrugged. "Taylor's traveling in Asia next week so I probably won't get to talk with him 'til Friday. I'll call and tell you whatever else he discovers. . . Shrimp are exceptional," Rick said, changing the subject. "Where'd you find such nice big ones with the heads still on?"

"Just the regular market where I always shop; this is New York you know, you can get everything in New York."

Rick nodded. "I don't cook for myself very often, but I'd have a tough time in D.C. getting fat shrimp like these with the heads on."

"I'm sure I'll be able to find whatever we want in Washington, after all, the D.C. Metro-area is quite a sophisticated place; I mean, with all the embassies and wealthy foreigners." She twirled some linguine on her fork while twisting her full lips into an impish grin.

Rick closed one eye and looked at Cyn with a confused expression. "I don't understand?"

As Cyn placed her fork on the plate and pushed back into the barstool, the silk dressing gown she'd hastily pulled on before she began to cook fell open, revealing a firm, medium-size breast with an upturned pink nipple. The tan lines of the skimpy bikini bra she'd worn last summer were still evident. She made no attempt to cover herself. "I'm taking a leave of absence from the museum, six months, maybe longer. I'm all packed up and I'm going back to Washington with you on Sunday night. We're going to be living together and I'm going to be your cook, chauffer, companion, cleaner, and full-time lover; mostly, your lover. Doctor Solomon thinks I'm ready, he gave me the go-ahead."

During Cyn's short speech, Rick's right hand and wine glass remained paralyzed, in midair. He hastily set the glass down on the granite, sending a knife clattering to the floor. "What, what are you talking about, and who in hell is Doctor Solomon?"

Cyn put both elbows on the countertop and leaned forward. "You were right, I have to admit, you were right. Four months ago I dumped Celia Rostenpoff and started treatment with Doctor Solomon. Solomon's a real psychiatrist, an MD. You know what he found out?"

Rick started at her, dumbfounded, without speaking.

"Don't you wanna know? I'll tell ya—I'm a loony, a certified loony. I have a mental disorder, it's like bipolar, but much more complicated; of course, if it's my disorder it would have to be more complicated, I don't do generic anything. Solomon fooled around with a number of medications for two months until he got the perfect combination; amazing what they can do now days. For the last two months I've been taking two blue capsules in the morning and a yellow one at night. He's kept me on a tight rein to see if my condition was really under control. I've had to keep a detailed behavioral diary, review it with him every other day, and phone in on weekends. This past Thursday he gave me the go-ahead to move back in with you; now, all I need is your okay."

Rick was shaking his head slowly from side to side. "I'm blown away; I don't know what to say to you."

"Ricky, it's like this. I still have the crazy upside in my personality, my behavior, that'll never change, that's me. The huge difference now is that when I come down from the highs, I do it slowly, gently; so slowly that I can recognize and manage the descent without hurting you or me in the process. That's what the medications do, it's amazing. You'll see, I'm a different woman, but still lots of fun."

Rick sighed. "What made you finally dump Celia, after I'd asked you to see a real doctor for years?"

"One night, after I'd worn out the second vibrator in a month, I came to my senses and realized that I'd always be a one-man woman, your woman. I also realized that things couldn't stay as they were, eventually you'd find someone else and I'd be lost, lost for the rest of my life. I asked Sally to help me find treatment; she told me about Solomon, he treats quite a few of the major-league wackos at MIT. I went to see him the next day."

"Why didn't you tell me about the treatment sooner?"

"Solomon wouldn't let me; 'one step at a time,' he said."

Rick forcefully placed both palms on the granite top and stared intently into Cyn's brown eyes. "What if I came here tonight to tell you that we couldn't meet like this anymore?"

Cynthia bit her lip and lowered her head.

"You should have told me sooner, Cyn. I mean, I haven't; I haven't found someone else. But what if I had? The two of us would be in loveless misery for the rest of our lives."

Cynthia sat up straight and smiled. "Can I take that as a yes?"

SEVEN

In a fashionable cul-de-sac just off Berkeley Square, tucked between an antiquarian bookseller and a high-end real-estate agent, were the London offices of Donner Systems Corporation. The early nineteenth-century town houses along the well-maintained, semicircular row were originally built as London residences for country landowners and wealthy merchants. The real estate was now far too valuable for residential use, and the former town houses had become offices for specialist businesses, a foreign ministry, and home to an elegant French restaurant.

As with all Donner Systems facilities, there were no signs on the London office to identify the corporate occupants or the nature of their business. A heavy, dark-blue front door led into a compact, newly renovated reception area; to the back was a small elevator with polished, brass-colored doors; to the side, an oak staircase with well-worn treads and an obviously newer banister. Concealed surveillance cameras focused on the unmanned reception area, the building entrance, and the elevator, and panned the street outside. During office hours, the cameras were monitored by an armed security team on the second floor. In the evening, the cameras were cut over to a contract surveillance firm. Eighteen months ago there had been a nasty incident—a young, bearded male had pulled up to the front door on a DHL delivery motorbike. The receptionist saw his DHL uniform on her monitor and buzzed him in. When he placed the package he carried on her desk, it exploded, killing them both and spraying the walls and floors with their blood and body parts. The story was plastered on the front page of the evening tabloids and prominently featured on the evening TV news. By the next morning, British government agencies had helped the investigating police conclude that the bombing was a tragic case of mistaken identity; the bomb was actually intended for a diplomatic mission with a similar address, on the other side of the cul-de-sac, not the offices of the Canadian export-import business where it exploded. . . Nicholas Donner knew better; the bomb was a warning.

* * *

Matilda Crane opened the door to the third-floor library and escorted Martin Jasper to the unoccupied chair at the circular oak table in the middle of the room. Jasper pulled on the lapels of his suit jacket and vigorously shook his head before sitting. "Bloody London Transport," he exploded. "Train broke down just short of the platform; took them an hour to sort it out." He looked up at Matty. "I trust you got my message?"

"Matty informed us of your predicament," Donner replied on her behalf.

Jimmy entered the room and discreetly placed a black folder in front of each of the four men seated at the table.

"Would you like coffee or tea?" Matty asked Doctor Donner.

"Gentlemen?"

Fidel and Avi declined; Jasper and Donner asked for coffee.

Three of the four men watched Matty's shapely rear follow Jimmy across the parquet floor and disappear through the door.

"It's a crime against nature to put a great ass like that in a tight, leather skirt," Fidel groaned.

Donner clicked his tongue. "She'd break you in two, Fidel, like a twig. Black belts in karate and Muay Thai, whatever that is."

"Shall we?" Doctor Donner asked as he broke the silver seal on the folder in front of him.

The others followed Donner's lead, unsealing their folders. Matty knocked and then pushed a stainless-steel cart with insulated carafes of coffee and hot water into the room. She started to serve the coffee, but Doctor Donner dismissed her with a polite nod of his head and wave of his hand. "I'll take care of that," he said with a smile.

"As you wish," she replied somewhat curtly, and retreated, this time without the following stares.

The men read in silence for nearly twenty minutes. General Thornton was the first to speak. "Damn fine work!" He slapped his hand on the table causing Jasper's coffee cup to jump in its delicate china saucer. "Avi, the dry-test results are brilliant."

Avi grinned. "According to the tracers, we'll get even more radiological dispersion than originally specified. And, we're well within the weight goals. Only task remaining is to load the fruit before deployment. I take it that'll happen on-site?"

The doctor and the General exchanged glances. "That's correct," Donner replied. "Fidel wants to ship the device and the fruit separately."

Avi nodded. "Makes sense, simplify the shielding requirements for shipping."

"Exactly," was all that Fidel offered.

Donner turned toward Jasper. "You're confident about the paper trail; difficult but not impossible to follow?"

"They'll discover the first leg from Iran to Caracas with only moderate effort. A Hezbollah operative will be clearly implicated in obtaining the fruit from Iran; he'll be off-line by then."

Fidel snorted. "You mean dead?"

"Off-line, as in unable to communicate," Jasper calmly replied, tapping his pen on the table. "The second leg, from Caracas to the factory will be more troublesome for them to follow; but, by then, they'll be onto the scent like an excited bloodhound and will plunge ahead." Jasper looked up toward Avi. "There's still an unresolved issue: Do we close the Nabatieh manufacturing operation before it's discovered or wait for them to find it? Letting them find it would be far more convincing, but, with the obvious collateral damage; Avi?"

Avi shrugged. "As you say, it's unresolved; it's on the list."

Jasper continued, "Once Thornton provides the target details and timing, I'll complete the paper trail—next meeting?"

"Final meeting," Doctor Donner replied with a broad grin. He cleared his throat. "Fidel, you go over transport first and then I'll discuss deployment."

General Thornton pushed back into his antique mahogany armchair. "As you're well aware, our window is November fourth through seventh. We're targeting the earlier end. Next month the device will be shipped out by ordinary airfreight. It'll be disguised to look like a high-tech medical device, part of a shipment of sophisticated medical equipment. As a precaution, a backup will ship to a separate location a day later. The fruit will be moved through unconventional channels to Egypt; it'll be packed in separate containers. From Egypt, the containers will move to the target site arriving only a day before planned detonation."

"There's no backup for the fruit?" Avi interrupted.

"Only the banana," Fidel replied. "If the rest of the fruit's compromised, we ship the spare banana and detonate with only the Strontium-90. Worst case, we detonate the explosive without the radiologicals. Not satisfactory, of course, but better than complete failure."

"Your confidence level?" Donner asked.

"For the device, very high; all of the links in the delivery chain are personally known to me. The medical equipment shipment will arrive at its destination as ordered and with every item on the waybill accounted for; the device gets separated from its disguise only after delivery. Obviously, the fruit presents a different set of challenges; radioactive leakage, weight, and size concerns among them. I'm quickly gaining confidence, however, that our strategy will be executed as planned and on schedule. I'll have specific details soon; the information you need for the paper trail, Jasper."

Doctor Donner nodded thoughtfully, and rose to his feet. "I need a bathroom break," he announced. "Jimmy has something for you to read while I'm out of the room." He opened the door and motioned to Jimmy. "Can you please distribute the report?"

By the time Doctor Donner had resumed his seat; the three men had broken the seal and finished reading the second document.

"Wasted a lot of time and money on this," Donner said with a grin. "Academics, social scientists; at my age, I should have known better. That said, I think we've finally got this nailed. Let's go down the list. Obviously, we're looking for a man; a big man, capable of carrying thirty kilos for a half mile."

"Twenty-six kilos." Avi beamed.

"Right, Avi, twenty-six kilos. How much is that in pounds and ounces?"

"A little over fifty-five pounds," Avi responded.

Donner nodded. "So we need a tall, strong guy who's slim enough so that the device will look like a pot belly under his robe—what's that called, Jasper?"

"In the Arabian peninsula it's a *thawb*."

"My high-paid scholars say he should appear Aryan as opposed to Semitic—Jasper, you can tell the two apart?"

"About seventy percent of the time; it's an acquired skill."

"Acquired skill," Donner repeated mockingly. "So far, we're looking for a tall, strong, trim man who looks Aryan rather than Semitic, at least to Jasper."

"Don't forget circumcised," Jasper said with a grin.

Donner shook his head. "You've read the psychological profile; two characteristics dominate. One, our man needs to be angry, very angry with Muslims, with Islam and filled with hatred, seeking revenge."

"Angry enough to kill," Fidel said.

"Second, our man must place little value on his own life. He must be ready to die; not die for jihad or Jesus but die because it's what he wants to do. Frankly, if we find an angry man who fits the physical profile and who's looking for death, the rest of the sociologist crap in the profile won't matter. I've got a team searching for that man right now. I expect to introduce him to you in September, at our last meeting."

"Nick, we're running late and Avi and I have a plane to catch. Can we get to the list?"

Donner nodded. "I think we've finished, haven't we? The punch list's become quite short. Anything I've missed?"

Avi cleared his throat. "Only the item Jasper raised, the Nabatieh manufacturing facility."

"And?" Donner asked.

Avi looked around the table.

Jasper's pale-blue eyes locked with Avi's. "We let them find it in operation," Jasper said. "It's the final piece in the puzzle; they won't be able to explain away the unambiguous Iranian connection."

Avi turned his gaze away from Jasper, his jaw was clenched and his lips drawn tightly together. "Jasper's right," was all he said.

While the four men said their farewells, Jimmy collected the black file folders and the copies of Donner's report. "Limo's here," Jimmy quietly told Doctor Donner. "Kurt's checked out the driver, he's one of ours."

Donner nodded and turned to Fidel and Avi. "Your car's arrived."

Matty retrieved the cups and spoons and wheeled the cart out of the library.

Fidel and Avi shook hands with Matty, and then followed Jimmy down the stairs to the waiting "hardened" Daimler limo that would take them to an RAF airfield outside of London and the DSC company jet.

Doctor Donner closed the library door, moved to the opposite side of the table, and rested his hands on a chair back. "Everyone's arrived?" he asked.

Jasper nodded. "Everyone; I've arranged a buffet for seven-thirty; no alcohol."

Donner grinned. "I know for a fact that two of the five will want a Martini; but, you're right, no sense giving offense to the others over a drink. The suite's clean?"

Jasper nodded again. "Your men have been there since yesterday, doing whatever it is they do."

"The Custodian's representative is prepared to take the lead?"

"He is," Jasper replied. "I spoke with his assistant this morning; everything's as agreed."

"You never cease to amaze me," Donner said with a grin.

Jasper stood. "End of the line, Nicholas, last project for me, forever."

"And then?"

"Martin Jasper, the old bugger, ceases to exist and I vanish into the Philippine sunset, lights dim, guitars softly fade away, just like at the end of a Spaghetti Western; and you?"

Donner grinned, lowered himself into a chair and pointed to another. "Sit down for a minute, Martin; some coffee, glass of wine?"

"Wine might be nice; any more of that nineteen-seventy Petrus about?"

"Most likely, besides you, Taylor and his friends are the only ones who drink what's in the cellar here. Ask Matty to send Jimmy down for a look."

Jasper strode to the outer office and quickly returned. "Jimmy was out there with Matty. He's gone to the cellar; I told him we'd need two glasses, right?"

"Yes, I'll join you; too soon to celebrate but lots to be optimistic about."

Jasper slid into the chair across from Donner. "And so, what will you do when this is over?"

"Give Taylor the reins, to start with. He already runs the company, of course, but I'll retire and let him get on with it, officially."

"I'm gobsmacked! I'm told the DSC office pool has you staying on until you're eighty!"

Donner laughed loudly. "Then I'll have to get my bet in soon, won't I?"

"Seriously, Nicholas, I can't see you sailing around in your boat for the rest of your life; maybe an appointment, ambassador to an out-of-the-way country, a place no one much cares about? Surely, they owe you that."

"Hah!" Donner exclaimed. "No President would ever trust me to make nice, especially this one. Diplomacy, Martin, power diplomacy, that's what's been lost, forgotten by this current lot. Keep everyone off balance, friends and foes alike. Don't ever let any of them know where you really stand, what actions you're likely to take. Reagan was the last President to understand the uses of power. You know how he destroyed the Soviet Union, don't you?"

"Common wisdom is that Reagan got the Russians into a hugely expensive arms race that depleted their resources from what they needed to hold their empire together."

"Poppycock!" Donner exploded with a smile. "The arms race was only part of Reagan's strategy; it was oil, oil and natural gas that finished the Soviets off. Reagan starved the Russians all right; he got the Saudis and the Gulf States to keep pumping and continue pricing oil in dollars; that kept the price of oil unnaturally low, and the dollar strong. In exchange, Reagan promised to provide the muscle to keep the House of Saud in power. Reagan knew that with the Soviets' massive energy deposits, they depended on the continuing rise of energy prices to hold their nasty little empire together. When energy prices stayed steady, and the dollar stayed strong, the Russians couldn't afford the costs to run their communist Ponzi scheme and keep all the client states in line at the same time."

Jimmy knocked, and then opened the library door. He entered

with a crystal decanter and two wine glasses in hand. "Petrus, nineteen-seventy; only four more bottles left," Jimmy announced. "Taylor must have been doing lots of entertaining, there was nearly a case of this when we were here in February." He placed the decanter on the table next to Doctor Donner and set a glass in front of each man.

Donner pushed the decanter toward Jasper. "You pour the wine," he said.

Jimmy left the room and closed the door behind while Jasper half filled the two glasses then raised his to his nose and breathed in deeply. "Taylor certainly knows his wines, this is ethereal."

"Martin, as you know there's a saying in the tribal Middle East that the enemy of my enemy is my friend. We're about to turn that saying on its ear and make the ancient enemy of our friends everyone's enemy." Donner raised his glass. "To the success of our executive action and a forced return to power diplomacy."

"Hear, hear," Jasper responded as the two men clinked glasses.

EIGHT

Mu lifted the two cloth carrier bags from the floor to the kitchen counter. The third bag was heavy and took two hands; the teenaged check-out clerk had carelessly packed a gallon of milk and two dozen cans of cat food in one bag. She looked at the assortment of cat food: shrimp and white fish, tender beef morsels in gravy, sliced turkey. *That cat eats better than we do,* she thought to herself. She placed her purchases in the pantry and the fridge, and then took the toothpaste, Q-tips, and mouthwash to the bedroom. The drapes were closed against the late-afternoon sun, and Rusty, asleep in bed on his stomach, was lightly snoring. As usual, Tater-Two was snuggled in a tight ball between Rusty's legs. Mu tiptoed to the bathroom and left the toothpaste and other items on the countertop. She quietly went back out through the bedroom and soundlessly closed the door. It was only four-thirty; Rusty could enjoy another hour and a half of rest.

Back in the kitchen, Mu read Rusty's note, then counted out the forty-five dollars sticking out from the pad. *This'll help buy Patsy's children's school clothes,* she thought. She folded the money in her hand and picked up the cream-colored envelope on top of the stack of mail that Rusty had left on the counter. Mu immediately recognized the compact, masculine handwriting; the envelope was postmarked New York. She carried it to her desk in the living room and placed Rusty's money under a corner of the desk blotter; she'd send a check to Patsy in the morning and then deposit the money in the bank after work. She knew that with Kyle out of work, Patsy needed all the help she could get.

Mu stared at the cream-colored envelope. She knew what it contained; Robbie had told her to expect the wedding invitation when he called the week before. She sighed and turned to look at the nine photos on the mantelpiece; nine young children, five girls and four boys. Except for the larger, cap-and-gown high-school graduation photo of a smiling, dark-haired boy, the other eight were all small, framed school photos—photos of children from six to fourteen years old, children with an assortment of brown and blue eyes, various skin hues, and a range of hair colors. All different hair colors, except for the photo of a frail-looking little girl prominently positioned in the center of the grouping; she had no hair or eyebrows, only the faint, enigmatic smile of an old-master painting.

Mu lowered her head; they were all her children and yet, not a one belonged to her. Two years after they were married, Mu and Rusty learned they were unlikely to have children. As they usually did, they accepted what life offered and chose not to pursue medical treatment for infertility; they never knew for sure, nor did they want to know, which of the two of them had a problem. Mu explored adoption; Rusty was supportive of her efforts, and they were about to place their names on a waiting list for an infant when Carol-Lee entered their lives.

Carol-Lee's young mother had died of an overdose. She'd been an addict since before Carol-Lee was born and most likely a prostitute as well. The Florida Family Services Department couldn't find a trace of Carol-Lee's father or any relative of her dead mother other than a stepbrother who was doing twenty years in a Texas state prison.

The Reverend Tony Jiggs was the pastor of Mu's church. He and his wife, Megan, took in foster children and helped Family Services find temporary families for at-risk children while the courts and bureaucracy decided on their long-term custody. At the time, in addition to their own twin boys, the Jiggs were fostering a teenage boy and could provide only a cot for Carol-Lee in Megan's sewing room on a short-term, emergency basis; the alternative was an orphanage.

Carol-Lee was six and small for her age. She had fine, wispy, blond hair, intensely blue eyes, and delicate, full lips that gave her frequent smiles a hypnotic quality.

Megan easily convinced Mu to provide an emergency foster home for Carol-Lee for a month or two while Family Services located a more permanent placement and, without any coaxing, Rusty agreed to put the child up in the spare bedroom. Rusty met Carol-Lee the next day at an after-school playgroup in the church basement. A half-dozen young children were playing tag, rushing from the safety of one wall to another while a small boy in the middle tried to tag the laughing, squealing children. Megan escorted Mu and Rusty into the basement room. Carol-Lee had met Mu the previous afternoon and waved to her. Rusty hung back just inside the door, he knew from past experiences with his niece and nephews that small children were often initially intimidated by his large body and deep voice, and waited for Mu to make an introduction.

"Time out," Carol-Lee called. She walked past Mu and Megan to Rusty and stood by his side. "I'm Carol-Lee," she said, looking up. "My new mom said you would be my daddy; I've never had a daddy before." She reached up and took his large hand. "You're big!" She smiled.

From that moment, Rusty and Carol-Lee were inseparable. With Megan Jiggs' assistance, Rusty and Mu extended the emergency fostering to permanent fostering. Three months later they hired a lawyer and were in the initial stages of adopting Carol-Lee when her illness began; she was diagnosed with leukemia. After nine months, Mu and Rusty, with the financial support of Family Services, had exhausted all the possibilities that modern medicine could offer; Carol-Lee died at home, in hospice care, her small hand entwined with Rusty's when she took her last breath.

It took a year before Rusty could force himself to agree to take in another foster child; Timmo, a lanky, athletic, eleven-year-old whose parents had been killed in a boating accident. Family Services needed only a few months to approve Timmo's godmother's application for custody, and then he was off to her farm in Wisconsin. Patsy came next, then the twins, who were followed by three other foster children whose stays with the Samadis lasted from a few months to several years. Finally, there was Robbie.

At fourteen, Robbie was five-foot-ten and still growing. He'd moved in with Mu and Rusty after his accountant-turned-real-estate-developer parents were convicted of fraud, tax evasion, and assorted other charges and sentenced to seven to ten years in a federal prison. Family Services decided to choose a foster home for Robbie away from his family's home in the Panhandle so that he could avoid the negative publicity attached to his parents' crimes. They needn't have troubled; Robbie gloried in the infamy of his parents' misdeeds. By the end of his first week at Baron County High, all of the students and teachers knew about the new boy's criminal parents. In his colorful retelling of their crimes and trial, Robbie cast Clarence and Marie Klep closer to the movie images of Bonnie and Clyde then to the greedy, money-grubbing accountants who'd systematically looted a string of small businesses and churches and invested their ill-gotten gains in rural property.

Robbie was an only child but had a string of uncles, aunts, and adult cousins he barely knew. They were scattered throughout Alabama, Florida, and southern Georgia. After his parents' trial, several of the relatives surfaced long enough to explore custody of Robbie, but, at sentencing, their enthusiasm quickly disappeared when all of Clarence and Marie's monies and worldly possessions were confiscated in punitive fines and repayments to the clients they'd defrauded. The only exception was an educational trust fund for Robbie that the court set aside for his college education.

Robbie was energetic and enthusiastic, and as honest and direct as Clarence and Marie were devious and secretive. Robbie and Mu bonded from the start. Robbie seldom mentioned his parents and consistently declined Rusty's regular offers to drive him to Coleman Federal Prison to visit. A month after he moved in, Robbie started calling Mu, Mom. Relationships developed more slowly between Robbie and Rusty; it took nearly six months for Rusty to agree that Robbie could drop the "foster" and introduce him to friends as "my dad." Shortly after, any remaining reserve vanished when Rusty found a story that Robbie had written for an English class; the paper was signed *Robert Samadi-Klep*. Rusty never missed a Baron County High football or basketball game while Robbie played on the teams.

Robbie was an excellent student but a far-from-perfect teenager; there were a few fights and a rowdy drinking incident in his high-school experience, but nothing serious, nothing the police officially recorded. He grew to over six-foot-two and with his dark hair and brown eyes, Robbie easily passed as Rusty and Mu's natural son.

Two months before Robbie turned eighteen and a month before high-school graduation, Robbie got a serious-looking letter from the State of Florida, a letter with an embossed gold seal on the envelope. The letter droned on for three legal-sized pages, but the message was simple. . .on his eighteenth birthday Robbie would no longer be a ward of the state, he was on his own.

Rusty and Mu received a similar letter from the State; it too contained a lot of words and a simple message; after Robbie's birthday they would cease to be his foster parents and their monthly support payments would end.

The letters changed nothing in their lives. Mu placed the two official envelopes in her desk drawer on top of Robbie's acceptance letter from Columbia University.

Rusty and Mu had put away one half of each monthly support check from Florida Family Services for the four years that Robbie lived with them, and on graduation day Rusty proudly presented Robbie with the keys to a late-model, low-mileage Mustang convertible and a check for four thousand dollars. Robbie spent some of the money on clothes for college, some for the lawyer and court costs to legally change his name to Robert Rustam Samadi, and put the rest in his bank account.

NINE

"Stop frettin', everything's covered. This isn't the first time Leo's taken over for you. There's never been a problem before, has there?" Mu set a plate of meat-loaf, mashed potatoes, and still-frozen peas on the plastic placemat in front of Rusty; it was his favorite meal.

"It's just Charley; ya know he has problems with anything that changes."

Mu carried a bowl of Rosa's chili to the table; she didn't much like meat-loaf. "Charley was just fine workin' with Leo when we went on the cruise last year. That was eight days; this time we'll only be gone for five." She opened the fridge and took out a pitcher of iced tea. "I made this tea up fresh. Would you rather have a soda, there's Diet Pepsi or ginger ale?"

Rusty nodded. "Iced tea's great, thanks; maybe with some lime?"

"I already put the lime in the pitcher, just the way you like."

Mu poured the iced tea into Rusty's insulated mug and into a tall glass for herself, and then sat at the table.

Rusty grinned. "Chili smells really spicy; maybe I could have a small spoonful?"

Mu shook her head. "Don't think so, especially not before a plane trip. Doctor said no spicy food for you until your GERD goes away. You haven't had bad indigestion since you been takin' the pills he gave you, have you?"

Rusty shook his head. "I thought it was GERT?"

"Nope, that pamphlet he gave you said GERD, stands for somethin' complicated, I don't remember."

"I been fine, the pills keep the fire out of my throat, but I sure do miss Rosa's chili."

"I picked up your dress trousers from the cleaners this afternoon; I want you to try 'em on after dinner with the jacket we bought. With the matching tie and dress shirt you're gonna look like a million bucks."

Rusty frowned. "One small problem; I don't think I can remember how ta tie a necktie."

"Got you covered, it's a clip-on."

"Good thinkin'! You get in enough food for Tater?"

"Stop frettin', Tater's gonna be just fine, Leo will be takin' good care of Tater the whole time we're away; you know how much Leo loves Tater. Now stop worryin'. I got the plane tickets for all three of us in my bag, along with Robbie's letter and the invitation. Rosa's gonna pick us up at ten tomorrow, she says that'll get us to the airport about two hours before the flight leaves, time for us to have some lunch; she says they only give you peanuts on planes now days. My first plane trip! I'm so excited. Now, if I could only get you to relax."

Rusty poured more iced tea for them both. "What did Robbie say they call Ina's father, I forget?"

"Robbie said to call him Max. His real name's Mooshie or Mushy or somethin' like that, but Ina told me everyone calls him Max. Robbie says that Max is down-to-earth and that you two will get along just fine."

"He writes books, this Max; I get that right?"

Mu nodded. "He's pretty famous. I got one of his books from the high-school library; I'll try an read it on the plane. Librarian says it's about the Palestinians and the Israelis."

"If this Max is anything like Ina, we'll get along fine. Ina's a sweetheart; with her blond hair and pale-blue eyes, she helps me imagine what a grown-up Carol-Lee would have looked like. Carol-Lee would be just about Ina's age, ya' know?"

Mu smiled. "I'm so happy for Robbie, Ina is a very special woman. Her mother's been dead for a long time; it's only Ina and her father living in New York City, or maybe it's New Jersey? Robbie and Ina are going to Israel for their honeymoon so that Robbie can meet the rest of the family, there's a lot of 'em, he said."

Mu took her bowl to the sink. "I'm so excited I can't eat any more, take your time; I'm gonna start packin' our suitcases. There's cherry cheesecake in the fridge for dessert, when you're ready."

Rusty grinned. "Haven't seen you this excited in years, like a little kid."

Mu placed her hands on Rusty's muscular shoulders. "My son's wedding in New York City, my first plane trip, new clothes, and a big party in a fancy New York Hotel; you bet I'm excited."

Rusty covered her hands with his. "Me too," he said with a big smile.

TEN

"Os, you're a sick dork!" Machala shouted as she slammed the apartment door in his face.

Os stood on the landing, glaring at the stained, paint-chipped door. It was as if Machala had purposely flipped a switch in Osman Kassim's disturbed mind; this was the moment when he turned his back on his twenty-two years in America and stared toward the blinding light of jihad in what he expected to be a brief, glorious finale to his thus-far wasted existence.

Like Os, Machala was the American-born child of refugees, hers from what she referred to as occupied Palestine, his from Pakistan. Machala was in the first year of a combined MS/PhD nursing program at New York University, while Os was an undergraduate, a senior, majoring in computer science. Machala was short and pudgy with full breasts, long, thick black hair, and hauntingly dark eyes. She'd been brought up in a middle-class, largely Muslim enclave in Queens. Her father was a family physician and her mother published and wrote for a weekly religious/political newspaper. Along with her two brothers, Machala was only moderately observant but frequented the Islamic Center as her parents required.

Os was from Dearborn, where his uncle and father owned a convenience store that operated as the first link in an organization transferring money from Michigan Pakistanis to individuals and militant organizations in and around Lahore. Os's mother died shortly after his birth, and he was raised by his grandmother, a loving but mentally sluggish older woman who never learned English and seldom left the house. Osman's father made sure that Os frequented the local mosque where he was nurtured in the teachings of the Prophet. The Islam that Os learned at home, however, was more likely to be expressed in the form of anger and threats of retribution toward the enemies of

Pakistan and Islam, rather than submission to the will of Allah. Os was an exceptional math and physics student and with the support of his high-school teachers, won a full scholarship to New York University in New York City.

Os and Machala met at a campus Islamic discussion group where Os's unyielding, often unfocused, anger was quickly leading to his isolation from the members of the group. Machala thought that Os was cute and, unlike the rest of the discussion-group members, found his unsophisticated, verbal histrionics amusing. She invited him to her apartment for coffee and after dissecting the anti-Muslim bias in the American media for a half hour, they moved to Machala's soft bed.

"He's okay, nice body, not much technique," she told a girlfriend the next day. "But then, the last thing I need in my life is a serious lover. Os can be my sex buddy, help keep my carnal desires in check. Someone clean and uncomplicated; he'll do for now."

When Abdulah had returned to New York from one of his frequent trips out of the area, he'd been freaked out by Machala's sudden appearance in Os's life. Os was approaching the critical stage of his conditioning, and Abdulah didn't need Os to have any distractions, particularly the distraction of frequent sex with the same woman, which could easily morph into some form of romance. Abdulah needed to have Os's full emotional attention.

Abdulah had followed Os for two weeks before he first spoke to him during prayers at the Islamic Center. "Weren't you ever taught the correct way to pray, or are you just lazy?" Abdulah chided. "Like this," he demonstrated. "Your forehead must touch the floor, each time." After prayers, Os followed Abdulah to a secluded corner of a local coffee shop where they talked for two hours until the shop closed and the proprietor told them to leave. Os gave Abdulah his address and they agreed to meet the following evening.

Os lived in a cramped studio apartment with multiple

computers and communications equipment packed around the unmade bed, the compact writing desk, and the lone chair. After his first visit to the apartment, Abdulah became a regular guest who would arrive at Os's door in the late evening with pizza or fast food in hand. The two of them would spend hours surfing jihadist Internet sites and blogs. Abdulah had been born in Egypt and was fluent in Arabic. He translated the Internet text and conversations with dramatic flair. When Abdulah's violent, jihadist blog was blocked, Os helped Abdulah polish and restructure the content and then shifted the blog to a new server and website; Os had Abdulah back online in less than a week.

Os was proud of how he'd transformed Abdulah's unstructured video collection of grizzly corpses, alleged victims of infidel atrocities, into a logically ordered story that could guide a viewer's emotional reactions from disgust to outright rage. Os labored for twelve hours without food or rest on a script that plumbed the depths of Muslim emotions and climaxed by exhorting the faithful to jihad and the rewards of paradise. With Abdulah's emotional Arabic rendering of Os's powerful script, complete with English subtitles, the blog drew heavy hits and comments. Os was proud of his work, he wanted Machala to see the professionally presented message he'd created; a message she'd understand and resonate with. He burned a DVD for her, a tribute to his growing affection.

Five minutes into the gory display of armless and legless children and twisted corpses with horrific wounds, Machala bounded from the couch and roughly turned off the TV. She ejected the DVD and threw it, like a Frisbee, at Os's head. "That's crap, Os, that's disgusting, sick crap! I think you should take your crap and get out of here."

Os was stunned; he expected Machala to approve, to be proud of his work. He stumbled to his feet, upending a can of Dr. Pepper onto the patterned carpet as he stood. "But it's real, it's true," he shouted.

"You're sick, Os," she said while violently shaking her head. "I'm an American, an American citizen; I'm also a Muslim woman. It sickens me that soldiers from my country are killing my sisters and brothers in Iraq and Afghanistan, but this is my country, I have to find a way to live with it. I don't want you coming here anymore, you understand?" She grabbed Os's dark-blue hoodie from the arm of the couch and threw it in his general direction. He turned to argue with her but saw from her indignant expression that there was nothing to discuss.

The next night Abdulah explained; Os had misunderstood Machala's passion, Os's and Machala's frequent, emotional discussions, discussions that often intruded into their sleep and study hours, were actually unrelated parallel conversations. Machala was focused like a laser on a target. First she would get her PhD in nursing; then, with her mother's help, she would gather the backing and financial assistance to establish a medical clinic in New York City, a clinic for poor Muslim children. Over time, her clinic would establish branches throughout the country, and Machala and her parents would be honored within the American Muslim community.

Abdulah guided Os to understand that Machala's anger, the disgust she expressed for the infidels who killed and maimed the children of Islam and drove them from their lands, was a woman's anger. Her thoughts were of healing and soothing wounds, not exacting revenge and retribution as a man would do; men lived and fought in the present. A woman could never comprehend a man's rage.

"For a true believer, life is a long punishment; but life can also be the door to a glorious eternity in paradise," Abdulah said quietly, his lips next to Os's ear.

ELEVEN

Os had his doubts about New Jersey; he wasn't sure there really was such a place. In his limited experience, the place called New Jersey was a maze of crowded roads, a space people traveled through to get from somewhere to somewhere else; not a place where humans actually lived. The New Jersey Turnpike, Garden State Parkway, Palisades Parkway, Atlantic City Expressway, and innumerable interstates connected New York with Philadelphia; New England with I-95, Delaware, Washington and the South; and the mid-state connection with the Pennsylvania Turnpike led from New Jersey to Ohio, Chicago, and the West, and vice versa. Not counting highway rest stops and gas stations, Os was sure that few people had ever set foot in the place called New Jersey.

Os maneuvered the rented Malibu through the Holland Tunnel, then south on the Garden State Parkway, and west on I-280, without sighting significant instances of habitation. Only when the female who lived in the GPS satellite navigation device told him to exit I-280 onto Becker Farm Road in Roseland, did Os begin to believe in New Jersey. There were office buildings and a church and then a gas station and a florist shop at the intersection; just like a real town. Her voice directed him a half mile farther, through three turns, to an older, well-maintained, ivy-covered bungalow. He parked the car in the driveway and climbed the steps to the screen porch where a woman was waiting for him in the open doorway.

She smelled of garlic; her whole house smelled of garlic. Her kitchen reminded Os of his grandmother's ancient kitchen in Dearborn: white enameled cabinets that had absorbed decades of airborne grease and turned to a putrid ivory color; an old, but sparkling Sears' Kenmore oven/range; a white porcelain sink, with dark chips showing through the enamel in several places; and a wire draining rack. The similarity with the Dearborn home was not a fond memory. Unlike his shrunken, brown, boney grandmother, this woman was middle aged, olive skinned, and fat; probably Italian or Spanish, Os thought.

The woman took a shoebox from a lower cupboard and placed it on the Formica-topped table. "I think one of these will suit you," she said, as she removed two handguns and carefully, almost reverently, placed them on the clean dish towel she'd laid on the table in front of Os. Except for a slight difference in size, the weapons looked identical. She pointed to the pistol closest to Os: "Glock twenty-six, semi-automatic, ten-round capacity. For you, this one's eight hundred." She turned her attention to the second. "This is a Glock seventeen-C, brand new, seventeen rounds; it's twelve hundred—that includes a concealed carry holster. I'll throw in a couple boxes of hollow-point cartridges with either one; cash and carry, of course. Pick 'em up; see which one feels the best to you. Don't worry, they're not loaded."

Os had never handled a firearm before, not even a toy pistol. He gingerly picked up the model 17-C and aimed it at the chain dangling from the exhaust fan set into the wall above the stove. "I'll take this one," he said in a near whisper.

The woman nodded. "You don't know much about guns, do you?"

Os shook his head.

"You made a good choice," she said, as she wrapped the unsold model 26 in a felt cloth, placed it back in the shoe box, and returned the box to the cupboard. "I store the ammunition in the parlor cabinet. I'll get a couple boxes and then show you how to load it and how to work the safety."

"Thanks," Os replied.

When the woman returned with the ammunition and the holster, she found ten 100 dollar bills and four 50s neatly arranged on the table.

She pocketed the money and sat on the soon-to-be-antique, chrome, pink and gray, padded kitchen chair next to Os. She removed the empty clip from the pistol. "Like this," she said.

"Just load it for me and show me how to take the safety off," Os replied. "I won't need the rest of the bullets; I'm only going to use it once."

TWELVE

The two attractive, well-dressed women sat across the table from each other like Queens on a chessboard. Cynthia the Red Queen: her long auburn hair, friendly chestnut-brown eyes, and trim body wrapped in an off-the-shoulder crimson dress. Gillian the White Queen: her short, casually styled, natural blond hair, pale-blue eyes, and off-white, spaghetti-strap sheath dress, appropriate to the part.

Soft light from the three outsized candelabra on the sideboard reflected off the large diamonds in Gillian's tennis bracelet, casting flashes of fire on the white linen tablecloth.

"I'm so happy you're living in the District, now at last maybe we can become good friends?" Gilly's speech was flavored with an odd mix of her native British and transplanted Massachusetts accents, along with a hint of Southern drawl; the drawl had been acquired only since she and Taylor and the twins moved to the Fairfax County, Virginia, horse farm. "I know there isn't a whole lot we have in common, except for Taylor and the fact that we share the same last name, but I'd make a good friend; I've always admired you, you and your brilliant career."

Cyn grinned and gently shook her head. "Actually, I'm not going to be a Donner anymore, I've become Cynthia Cappa; I'll only be Doctor Cynthia Donner for professional appearances, infrequent professional appearances." Cyn reached across the table and placed her hand over Gillian's perfectly manicured and polished fingers. "Gilly, I know that you're a good person and a great wife for my brother. I was pleased, really pleased when you two married. Taylor needs a wife, a loving wife; loving doesn't come easily to Taylor or to me. I think the two of us are missing some important emotional genes; our father was always kind to us, but never loving. I know that Taylor adores you, and Ricky tells me that the twins have taken to you as well, he says that

Nicko's started calling you 'Mom.'"

Gilly smiled and blushed at the same time, the color rising in her Devonshire, peaches-and-cream complexion. "Nicola's a sweet child; I love her dearly. As you know, Patrick was very close to his mother, he's warm and respectful to me, but there's still a reserve. Nicko thinks that Patrick feels that if he shows too much affection toward me, he'll betray the love he carries for Elaine. Nicko told me that she and Patrick have discussed his feelings and that I should just wait for Patrick to come around; I think she's right."

Cyn patted Gilly's hand. "I'm sure she is."

"What are you going to do with yourself now that you're not with the museum full-time; can't picture you as a bridge-addicted, neurotic housewife?"

Cyn brushed her dark hair away from her face. "Making Ricky and me blissfully happy is my highest priority. Then, I'm going to finish the book I've been writing, struggling with, for the past ten years—the compendium of everything I've ever learned during my intimate life journey with the irascible Paul Gauguin. Some former colleagues at the National Gallery have asked for my help pulling together the new catalog of their wonderful Impressionist collection, and I'll still be on call to help the staff at the Museum of Fine Arts. Plus, an old friend wants my unofficial assistance in helping him document the initial collection of the new African American Museum. All that should keep me out of trouble and boredom for the next few years."

"You're planning on staying at the condo? The reason I ask is that there's a lovely old farm on our road that's just come up for sale; Taylor says that it'll sell for a fraction of what it'd really be worth in a more buoyant market. Wouldn't it be fun to be neighbors? We could ride together, Taylor brags about your horsemanship."

Cynthia gently smiled. "Afraid I'm an inveterate city girl. Except for the time I spent on sabbatical in Tahiti, I've always lived in a city: Boston, New York, Paris, and now Washington. Ricky and I have decided to redecorate the apartment and then, after we find something we like, we'll put it on the market. I'm gonna look for something a bit larger, a place where we can entertain, maybe a charming old brick townhouse in Georgetown or Foggy Bottom."

"What about your Beacon Hill property? Surely you're not going to part with such a magnificent home?"

Cyn shook her head. "My great-grandfather started construction on The Point in the eighteen-hundreds; when my mother left it to me she made me promise never to sell, to keep it in the family. It's a conundrum; perhaps when Ricky retires we'll move back, we both think of Boston as home. . . Doesn't pay to burn all one's bridges, does it?"

A short, dark man in a tux entered the private dining room; he was guiding a considerably taller Taylor Donner by the arm, much like a tugboat shepherding a freighter. "Look who I found," he grinned. "As you suspected, hiding on The Porch."

"Okay, Gus, you can stop twisting my arm now," Taylor ingenuously complained.

Gus bowed his head toward Gillian. "M'lady," he said, then turned on his heel and exited.

Taylor stood behind Gillian, placed his hands on her bare shoulders, bent and kissed her on the neck. "Sorry, darlin', I was just about to make my way to the table when the Gestapo collared me."

Gilly covered his hand with her own. "Gus does have a flair for the dramatic; I simply asked him to keep an eye out for you."

"My baby sister, beautiful, and a baby no more," Taylor enthused as he circled around the table to Cyn. She stood and they touched cheek to cheek, twice, in the French manner. "I'm so pleased you could join us," he said, and held her chair while she resumed her seat. "Rick will be here any moment, he's parking the car; we were talking before Gus took my cell phone away."

Gilly turned her head toward Cyn. "No cell phones allowed in the dining room, not even in these private rooms; actually, no cell phones allowed anywhere in the Club except for the Porch."

"The porch?" Cyn questioned. "Isn't it too wet and steamy to stand outside making phone calls this time of year?"

Taylor grinned. "The Porch is a small bar and card room, it's inside the doors of the gentlemen's locker room, and off-limits to our lovely ladies. Up until the end of the Second World War, club membership was restricted to men; women weren't allowed on the golf course, and female guests were permitted in the dining room only on weekends. Now that the women run the place and take away our phones, the Porch is the last bastion of male chauvinism."

"Poor, downtrodden wusses," Gilly laughed.

Rick Cappa bustled into the room, brushing raindrops from his dark hair with both hands. "Raining again, not really rain, more like a hundred percent humidity." He bent and kissed each of the women on the cheek and shook hands with Taylor. He sat and placed his hand over Cynthia's hand. "And how are you, my love?" he asked. Cyn smiled broadly and rubbed her knee against his leg in reply.

Their dinner was excellent: the main course, beef Wellington with foie gras. Each of the three courses was accompanied by a complementing wine, carefully chosen from the temperature-controlled wine storage unit Taylor maintained at the club and stocked for his private use.

When, with the dessert soufflé, Taylor reintroduced Gilly's earlier mention of the house for sale on the road where they lived, Cynthia quickly changed the subject. "Gilly said that you met with Father this morning. How is the old autocrat? I haven't seen him for a few months, not since his birthday party."

Taylor shrugged and nodded at the same time. "Strange meeting—mentally, Father seemed sharp as ever, but he's aging faster than I've noticed before. His cheeks seemed sunken in, and his chest and upper body are looking hollowed out. When I asked about his health, he said he was just fine, feeling good. He said that his quarterly medical was excellent; blood pressure, blood chemistry, weight, all unchanged and within the normal range."

"I've lost track, Nick's seventy-two now?" Rick asked.

"Seventy-four," Taylor replied.

"He still sails that big boat of his single-handed?"

"He does, of course it's fully automated, all electric winches, not much physical effort required; still, *Pandora*'s sixty feet and several tons of twitchy, nervous energy; one incredibly fast boat." Taylor paused and looked separately at each person seated around the table. "This has to stay private; the SEC would go apoplectic if what I'm about to tell you leaked out: Father's decided to step down and turn the company over to me, January first."

"I don't believe it!" Cynthia nearly shouted. "You sure this isn't a head fake, he's staying on the board?"

"Nope, said he wants to sever all ties with DSC, doesn't even want to be an advisor or consultant."

"Just like that?" Cyn asked. "Forty-six years of building and running the company, treating it like his personal fiefdom, maybe even plaything, and he says he can just walk away? Something's fishy, I don't believe it. What's he gonna do?"

Taylor shrugged. "That's the first question I asked. Father went strange, nearly freaked me out with his evasive reply."

"What do you mean, 'strange'?"

"Father's never been one to heap praise on either of his children."

Cyn grinned. "You can say that again; the only time in my life that I can remember him celebrating my accomplishments was when he unexpectedly showed up for my graduation, my PhD. Even then, he left early."

Taylor nodded. "So, I was blown away when he spent ten

minutes telling me how proud he was of Cynthia and Taylor; that's how he talked about us, 'Cynthia and Taylor,' like I was a third party, a friend of the family he was boasting to. He detailed all of Cyn's academic achievements, starting with prep school. Went on and on about her horsemanship, the events she'd won, the ribbons, the Olympic tryout. He talked about her monographs and TV appearances; he'd obviously read or seen most of them, the Gauguin retrospective she'd staged at the Museum of Fine Arts, and the glowing reviews—"

"I didn't think he even knew about the show!" Cyn interrupted.

"Oh, he knew," Taylor resumed. "After Cynthia, Father turned to 'Taylor.' Went lighter on the academic accomplishments, of course, but knew all the details of the deals and contracts that Taylor had won. Father said how well Taylor and Gillian were doing in raising and educating the twins. I sat there speechless, it was as if Father was giving a prepared speech; his words were obviously sincere, but curiously unemotional at the same time."

"This was after he announced that he was stepping down?" Rick asked.

"It was; what Father actually said about resigning was short and sweet. 'We both know that you've been successfully running this company for the last few years, running it without my help. DSC doesn't need me anymore and I don't need DSC either; it's all yours. Why don't you get the announcement ready for the first of January?' That was it."

"I don't want to appear argumentative," Rick began, "but won't Nick still be the largest shareholder, won't he still effectively control DSC?"

"On that point I'm sworn to secrecy. Father has some very interesting plans for his billions, plans that generously provide for everyone around this table, the twins and Sally as well; plans that will include DSC employees."

Gillian turned toward Taylor, she spoke slowly and softly, "Your father's acting like a man anticipating death."

Taylor nodded. "He is, isn't he; maybe even enjoying the anticipation."

THIRTEEN

Rick briskly accelerated his Corvette onto the on-ramp of the beltway; it was past ten and traffic had finally thinned.

"Ricky, I don't understand why Tay didn't want to talk about Father's secret activities in front of Gilly. I mean, he felt free to tell all of us about Father stepping down."

"Probably because Gilly and Nick don't get on," he said. "In my experience, Taylor rarely mentions your father in Gilly's presence. You know how awkward Nick was about their marriage, boycotting their wedding just because of her father's politics; I'm sure that Gilly's never forgiven him. Obviously, Taylor had to tell her about Nick stepping down; I think he just didn't feel that it was necessary for her to know about the bomb."

"Bomb!" Cyn shouted, "What bomb?"

"That's what they're doing—Nick and Fidel—they're building a small bomb."

"That's crazy! Father's a trained physicist, but he's hopelessly out of date with technology, he hasn't the faintest idea of how to build any kinda' bomb, and neither does Fidel. They're just two loony old men, that's what they are."

Rick shifted into sixth gear. "Maybe loonies, but rich and well-connected loonies. They're not building the bomb themselves; they're paying someone to do the job for them. Turns out you were wrong; Taylor does have someone inside your father's operation, not Kurt or Jimmy, but someone else, a woman. What do you know about Matilda Crane?"

Cyn shrugged. "Never heard of her."

"Officially, she's a well-paid, DSC executive assistant. Actually, she's a former Secret Service Agent. Taylor often uses her as a bodyguard, for himself and visiting executives or foreign government officials when they're traveling to or from a DSC office. She's been working with your father and keeping an eye on him for the past year. She alerted Taylor that something was going on about nine months ago. Two other men are involved along with Nick and Fidel. A Middle East type who calls himself Avi Tesla but has several other names, and a Brit, a minor aristocrat named Martin Jasper; that's his real name. Mrs. Crane isn't privy to the details of their meetings, but she came up with positive evidence that this Tesla character is having someone in the Middle East build a bomb, a small conventional bomb, not the nuclear type."

Cyn let out a deep sigh. "I knew it, I knew Fidel was bad news. What's Taylor gonna do?"

Traffic started to get heavier and Rick downshifted and slowed to fifty. "Taylor's theory is that they're gonna explode the bomb somewhere, then try to pin the blame on whichever Middle East faction or country they're targeting. He thinks they're trying to force the U.S. to act."

Cyn went rigid in the bucket seat. "Where would they detonate a bomb? Surely not in the U.S. or Europe! Father and Fidel are loonies, but they're also patriots with a capital P; they'd never purposely kill their own countrymen or allies; I'd stake my life on that."

"Taylor's in a difficult position. He doesn't feel that he can report his suspicions to any federal agency for a bunch of reasons; most important, he doesn't have any hard evidence. Mrs. Crane hasn't anything in writing, no evidence other than a few pages of documents she's read. Then there's the delicate matter of accusing his father and a respected, retired war hero. Finally, the possible damage to DSC's reputation; a scandal involving Nick and a bomb would destroy the company."

"Ricky, Taylor can't just sit on the information until a bomb goes off somewhere, can he?"

Rick shook his head. "He's had his people investigate this Avi Tesla and Martin Jasper; Taylor has two files on them. He's also tracking down all Nick's travel for the last few years. He's having a courier deliver copies of those files to me first thing tomorrow. Taylor wants me to read the files and then meet with this Mrs. Crane tomorrow evening, see if I can help get a better picture of what the group is planning."

"Why you?" she asked. "Why doesn't Tay hire a professional investigator?"

"Taylor's afraid to let anyone else near this; he can visualize his whole life, Donner Systems, and his reputation, slowly spiraling down the drain."

"When did Tay tell you all this?" she asked.

"On the phone, just before I arrived at the club for dinner tonight. Taylor didn't want me to tell you, but I told him that wasn't an option. Nick's your father. Besides, you have a sizeable financial interest in the continuing health of DSC. If I'm going to be involved in this, you have every right to know what's going on."

Cynthia leaned over and kissed him on the cheek. "You're right, two heads are always better than one. The courier's coming to the apartment or your office?"

"Our apartment, I thought it would be safer."

"I'll bake a crumb cake; we can have it for breakfast while we read the files."

Rick put his hand on her leg. "Crumb cake? You're getting a little carried away with this new homemaker persona, aren't you?"

Cyn grasped his wrist and moved his hand farther up on her leg. "You can help by lighting the oven," she purred.

FOURTEEN

Mu was bewildered, things weren't happening the way Robbie's letter said they would; inside the baggage hall, there were a dozen or more limo and taxi drivers holding signs, signs with names, but none that said SAMADI. The two margaritas she'd finished on the plane were adding to her confusion. She could see Rusty and Rosa standing next to the baggage carousel at the end of the hall, but no sign for SAMADI.

"Hey, Mom!" Robbie called out, tapping her shoulder. She turned into the arms of her son and almost daughter-in-law.

"Hey, Mom," Ina echoed. "Welcome to New York!"

Mu hugged them together and squealed with joy. Robbie kissed her on the nose. "Change of plans, we decided to pick you up ourselves; Max gave us his limo and driver for the weekend. . . Where are Dad and Aunt Rosa?"

Mu pointed toward the last carousel. "Getting our bags."

"Stay here with Ina," Robbie called over his shoulder as he jogged to the carousel, dodging the bodies and baggage in his path.

The carousel belt was moving, but empty. Rosa stared at the dark opening in the wall, a look of concern on her face. "You think they lost our suitcases?"

Robbie slid up behind the two of them and threw his arms around their shoulders. "Dad, Aunt Rosa!" he called. "I'm so happy to see you!"

* * *

Osman Kassim had positioned himself in the lobby on a cushioned rattan couch with an unobstructed view of the hotel's main entrance. He was neatly dressed in a dark-blue blazer, gray slacks, and blue oxford-cloth shirt, along with polished black tassel loafers; he held a copy of the *Wall Street Journal* at chest level. *Eden* was one of the trendy boutique hotels that were continually sprouting around the city. The lobby was a designer's clumsy interpretation of earthly paradise, abounding with exotic plants and flowers, padded benches, unique carved tables, and garden seats all arranged in intimate groupings among the foliage. The color scheme, soft greens and yellows with gold accents, supported the decorator's attempts at creating a place of calm and peace. The Serpent's Grill was discreetly out of view around the corner and to the side of the lobby, as were the three hotel elevators.

Os had followed Abdulah's instructions like an actor in a play. When he first entered the hotel he'd inquired of the stunning young woman behind the reception desk for the house phones. When Os asked the hotel operator for Moesha Trabar's room, he already knew that the room would be unoccupied; when the phone rang for the seventh time, and the operator asked if he would like to leave a message for Mister Trabar, Os said that he would wait in the lobby. Os went into the Serpent and looked up to the high ceiling at the skillfully executed reproduction of Michelangelo's Sistine Chapel painting of God passing the spark of life to Adam. When a waiter asked if he would like a table, Os told him that he was waiting for someone and retreated to the lobby. Os had established his legitimacy to occupy a seat in the lobby, at least for an hour or two.

Os felt the weight of the Glock riding in the holster against his left rib cage. He was calm and confident. Before he left the mosque, Abdulah had explained one last time: he, Osman Kassim, was the Hand of Allah, the hand that would carry out the *fatwa* against the Jew-pig Trabar, the blasphemer of the Prophet. "The Hand of Allah." Os repeated the phrase over and over in his mind.

* * *

"You have to promise not to tell anyone." Ina raised a finger to her lips. "Robbie and I were married on Tuesday in a civil ceremony!"

Rosa was visibly shocked. "But we've come for your wedding!"

Ina grinned. "You won't be disappointed, there's going to be a wedding, a lovely wedding, it just won't be the legal one."

"I don't understand." Mu was confused. "Why won't it be legal?"

Ina tossed her head. "It's like this, my father's a Jew and my mother was a Catholic. I was only three when Mother died. Nanny and my mother's sister conspired to see that I was educated in a convent school, made sure I'd be raised Christian; that spawned a lot of angst among the two sides of the family. To maintain harmony, our wedding ceremony will be performed jointly by a rabbi and an Episcopal priest, family friends. It's a bit complicated to explain, but neither has the legal authority to conduct a marriage in New York; sooo. . .we were married in the eyes of the law on Tuesday, and on Sunday, we'll be married with the blessing of the Gods."

"Double the blessings!" Robbie laughed, while he popped the champagne. "Hold on a sec, it gets bumpy on the bridge, don't want to spill any of this precious nectar."

"Don't think I should," Mu demurred, placing her fingers over the top of her glass. "I had two drinks on the plane and my head's real fuzzy."

Rosa extended her glass. "Fill 'er up! I don't expect I'll ever get the chance again to drink expensive wine in the back of a big black limo; you either, Muriel Samadi, drink up!"

The pothole-riddled bridge behind them, Robbie filled all their glasses.

"To my mom and dad, whose enduring love for each other is the example that'll guide me in my marriage."

"And to my son and his beautiful wife," Rusty added.

The five of them clinked glasses and sipped their champagne.

"And to my new aunt Rosa, as well," Ina proposed. "Max was coming to greet you at airport along with Robbie and me, but he got a call as we were leaving the hotel, he and Jacob had to go downtown. No matter, Max will join us for dinner tonight; there'll be just the six of us, plus Jacob, of course; Jacob is Max's bodyguard."

* * *

Os fished the cell phone from his jacket pocket. "Yes?" he answered.

"They'll be there soon: black limo, three women and two men. It's likely the younger man will enter first, he's the bodyguard: tall, slim, dark hair, denim jacket, a white tee shirt, and wearing sunglasses. The blasphemer, Trabar, is dark haired and tall as well. No confusing the two men, Trabar's more muscular with broad shoulders and lots older; in his fifties. He's wearing a brown jacket over a white collared shirt, no glasses." Abdulah paused. "Don't forget; get the bodyguard, the young guy first. Keep the gun under the newspaper until the last minute. Trabar will be unarmed, get within a few feet before you fire, and then empty the gun into his chest. Got that?"

"Right," he said.

"Drop the gun on the floor and walk out the door at a normal pace; turn right onto twenty-sixth, you'll see the van about six cars down, I'll be waiting—never forget, you are the Hand of Allah."

"I understand," Os replied and snapped the phone shut.

* * *

They'd opened a second bottle of Cordon Rouge; Mu had gotten into the spirit and kept up with the never-ending toasts.

When the limo turned onto the Avenue of the Americas, Ina helped Mu find her "flats" and slipped them onto Mu's feet just as the limo arrived at the front entrance to Eden. The driver came around to the passenger side and opened the door. Rosa was closest to the door and, with the driver's assistance, climbed out and onto the sidewalk. Ina was next; she and Rosa reached back into the limo, each grasped one of Mu's arms, and helped her to stand. Mu's head bumped against the door opening, mussing her new hairdo, but she didn't notice. Robbie exited, pocketing his cell phone as he stood. "Max called; things changed and he got back sooner than expected. He's coming up from the parking garage to the lobby just now to welcome everyone," he said to Ina.

Rusty slid across the backseat and climbed out with surprising grace for a large man; his oversized body had easily absorbed the champagne with no outward effects. Rosa and Ina curled their arms around Mu's waist and helped her toward the door.

"What about the bags?" Rusty asked Robbie.

"Driver'll bring them in," Robbie replied.

Robbie moved quickly to open one of the heavy plate-glass doors for the three women. Rusty followed and opened the other door. Robbie stepped into the vestibule and pulled open one of the two inner doors.

The events of the next twenty seconds would be indelibly etched into Rusty's memory where they would replay in an endless loop, for the remainder of his life. A young, dark-haired man moved toward Robbie as if to help Robbie hold the inner door, then, three ear-bursting explosions echoed through the serene, plant-filled lobby. Robbie's body jerked sharply to the left; another explosion, and, seemingly in slow motion, Robbie slid to the floor; while at the same instant, Mu's head jerked backward and bright red arterial blood pulsed from her throat, streaming down onto the pale-blue blouse she'd found on sale at Walmart. Mu grasped her spurting throat wound with both hands, as if trying to stop the copious blood flow, and then fell forward on top of Robbie. The next shot caught Rusty in the shoulder, pushing him backward into the second glass door. Three more shots came in rapid succession, striking Os in the back of the head. Os' legs crumpled and he tumbled, face first, onto the cold marble floor with a sickening crush of bone and teeth; the Glock fell from the hand of Allah, rattled on the floor, and settled next to Robbie's head in a gathering pool of blood.

FIFTEEN

Rosa sat rigid on the padded chair in the surgical waiting room. She was alone in the room and had switched off the blaring TV an hour ago. Other than the bubbling and gurgling from the filter in the fish tank across the room, the soft clicking of her rosary beads was the only sound. The blood stains on Rosa's mint-green slacks had dried to an unpleasant adobe red. Rosa silently mouthed the words of the Hail Marys and Our Fathers and stared uncomprehendingly at the brightly colored tropical fish.

Ina ran, literally ran, into the room and grasped Rosa's shoulders. "He's gonna make it!" Ina whispered through her sobs, tears flowing freely down her cheeks. "Robbie's gonna make it!"

Rosa stood and the two women embraced and wept together. "Thank you, dear Jesus!" Rosa rejoiced in a small quavering voice. "Thank you, Holy Mother!"

"He has a collapsed lung and his shoulder and ribs are all shot up, but he's gonna live!"

* * *

Nicholas Donner was at his desk in the Maryland retreat he and his staff called "the Cabin." The walls of his office were covered with awards, autographed photos, and framed letters of congratulations and thanks from U.S. Presidents, cabinet secretaries, congressional luminaries, foreign government leaders, and even a queen.

Donner was on the phone, he was smiling. "Johnston just called, he runs the selection committee. He said that the story's coming through on UPI; the networks haven't picked it up yet. This could be our man. His wife and son were murdered by a Muslim terrorist in a New York hotel, gunned down as they entered the lobby. UPI says it was probably a case of mistaken identity, the gunman thought that he was carrying out an Islamic death sentence, what's that called?"

"Fatwa," Martin Jasper replied. "Strictly speaking, a fatwa can be any ruling by a mufti; but, in the West, the term's usually applied to a death sentence."

"Right, a fatwa against Moesha Trabar."

"*The* Moesha Trabar, the Nobel prize winner?"

Donner nodded. "Yeah, that Trabar. Seems like Trabar's daughter was about to marry the son of this guy from Florida. Wait a minute." Donner looked at the notes he'd jotted on a yellow pad. "Samadi, that's the name of the guy whose wife and son were killed, Rustam Samadi."

"Hmmm, Samadi, probably Persian," Jasper interjected.

"UPI story is that Samadi and his son entered the hotel lobby with Ina Trabar, the writer's daughter, along with Samadi's wife and another woman. Since Samadi was with Trabar's daughter, the terrorist may have mistaken Samadi for Trabar and his son for Trabar's bodyguard."

"I saw Trabar lecture at Oxford, six or seven years ago; he was a big man, over six feet, so—"

Doctor Donner finished Jasper's thought. "So, if the gunman mistook this Samadi for Trabar, Samadi must be a big man."

"And, as I said, Samadi's likely a Persian name; Rustam, too. Samadi wasn't injured?"

"He was, but UPI says his injuries aren't life threatening."

"What happened to the gunman?" Jasper asked.

"Shot and killed. The real Trabar and his bodyguard were entering the lobby from the elevators at the other end when the shootings took place; the bodyguard shot the terrorist in the head, killing him instantly."

"We may have gotten lucky," Jasper said. "A big man, possibly of Persian origin, who's got to be seething with hatred against the people who killed his wife and son; it's almost too perfect to be plausible."

"Johnston's on the way to New York; I'll let you know after he calls. This could be our man."

"I'll be here all night and tomorrow as well," Jasper replied, and hung up.

* * *

It was a primal scream, an animal howl. The two veteran nurses looked up from the paperwork they were updating and sadly shook their heads. They'd heard the primitive wail before: the scream of a gull as her hatchlings were ripped from their nest in the talons of a hawk; the pitiful yelp of a fox, helplessly circling the steel trap where his vixen writhed in agony, her paw crushed by the trap's unyielding steel jaws. They knew the reason for the desperate howl; the big man in room 3307 had recovered consciousness and learned that his wife was dead.

SIXTEEN

Matilda Crane wasn't exactly beautiful, but, in the style of a voluptuous, pop star, she was undeniably sexy.

Cynthia watched Ricky's eyes explore Matty's assets: her shoulder-length red hair, wide-spaced, topaz-blue eyes, pouty lips, full breasts, slim waist, and sensual hips. Matty wore a fitted, black-velvet jumpsuit, the front zipper left low to reveal a golden starfish on a fine chain nestling between her breasts. Cyn silently congratulated herself on her decision to accompany Ricky to the meeting.

Matty's living room reflected a minimalist approach to decorating; two light cocoa–colored, suede leather couches were set perpendicular to each other facing a massive antique-looking credenza made of some sort of dark wood with a large flat-screen TV suspended on the wall above. Three large-format abstract paintings, done in earth tones, filled the remaining wall space. The side tables were hammered copper; a honey-colored bamboo floor lent a warm glow to what would otherwise have been a cold, stark room.

Introductions out of the way and a bottle of Merlot half finished, the three of them were seated on the suede couches animatedly discussing Nicholas Donner.

"The only thing you need to know to understand my father is that he's totally self-centered. Not self-centered as in selfish; Father's anything but selfish. It's just that he finds it impossible to consider opinions that differ from his own. It's not exactly arrogance; it's more like a flaw in his intellectual processing capabilities. The people in Father's inner circle, the ones who survive, aren't yes-men, but they *are* all men, men who genuinely agree with father's view of the world and—"

Rick interrupted. "Wealthy, powerful men."

"Right, wealthy men with lots of financial and political

influence," Cyn continued.

"I understand that your father's a big political supporter, mostly Republicans?"

Cynthia grinned. "Yes, he passes out lots of money, and no, about the Republicans. True he was close with Reagan and the first President Bush, but he was also an unofficial advisor and financial backer to Clinton and, after the first term, he wasn't exactly close with George W."

Rick nodded. "Almost all of DSC's revenue comes from U.S. or foreign governments, either directly or through subcontract relationships. The company has to spread its donations around. As DSC's founder and Chairman, Nick has to follow suit. Taylor does an excellent job of guiding the distribution of Nicholas Donner's personal millions."

"You're DSC's lobbyist?" Matty asked.

"My company provides that service to Donner Systems, as well as others."

Matty cocked her head. "How about General Thornton? Lecherous old sod pinched my butt; I made sure he wouldn't do it a second time."

Cynthia smiled. "Fidel's been one of my father's inner circle for as long as I can remember; often showed up at our Boston home when I was young, before my mother died. He got his hard-ass reputation in Vietnam and then during air commands in the Middle East and Europe. After that it was mostly staff jobs with NATO and the Joint Chiefs. Father once told me that Fidel has more worldwide IOUs due and payable than a pawnbroker."

"Fidel?" Matty asked.

Rick set his empty glass on the table. Matty reached for the bottle. "Not for me," he said, "although it's very good. . . No one knows why Thornton's called Fidel. I was once told that it has something to do with an ex-girlfriend. He's quite the ladies' man, never married."

"You've read the files on the other two?" Matty asked.

Cyn nodded. "Not all that much detail, but it still took most of the morning; like reading a spy novel without a plot."

Matty countered. "I can assure you, there's a plot. The challenge is to figure out what they're gonna do, and where, before they do it. In spite of all his pseudonyms, Tesla—aka Hurwitz, aka Schilling, aka Piffer—is probably the less complicated of the two. He's clearly a brilliant engineer, well educated, greedy, and for hire to whoever will pay his price: no politics, loyalties, or scruples. Is that how he comes across to you?"

Cyn twirled the wine in her glass. "I found the bit about his past connections and loyalties confusing. File said his parents were Lebanese, but that he worked for the Mossad for years. I thought the Lebanese and Israelis were bitter enemies?"

"That's what I meant about Tesla having no loyalties; the report made it clear that he's worked for the Russians and the Americans as well. How'd your father get to know him?"

Rick answered Matty's question, "Donner Systems work with all sorts of people around the world. Sometimes our government finds it more convenient for contractors like DSC to manage possibly problematic relationships. I never heard of Tesla before I read the files; you, Cyn?"

Cyn shook her head. "Never."

"Why don't you tell us about the bomb," Rick asked Matty. "We can talk about Martin Jasper afterward. I'm sure you didn't find out about a bomb from the files on Tesla and Jasper?"

"No, I didn't. Let's start at the beginning. Taylor sent me to work on Doctor D's staff nine months ago, mainly to protect Doctor D. There were some creditable threats of violence against DSC executives, and Taylor was concerned Kurt might be getting rusty. Taylor also told me to keep my eyes and ears open for anything out of the ordinary in the chairman's office. You both know Jimmy and Kurt, right?"

Cyn nodded. "Jimmy's worked for my father since I was a teenager; he was a guest at our wedding. Kurt joined father's staff about ten years ago, he was a Marine. They're both extremely loyal to my father."

Matty chuckled. "Kurt figured out that I wasn't the typical executive assistant and treated me like I was a likely assassin for the first few months, tried hard not to leave me alone with Doctor D. Jimmy came around a lot faster; a tight sweater, a pat on his arm, a coy smile; all tools of the trade."

"They teach you that in the Secret Service?" Cyn asked.

"I started learning in kindergarten, and you?"

Cyn laughed, she was beginning to warm to Matty. "I was a slow learner, probably seventh grade."

"Since I've been on Doctor D's staff, he's had three meetings with General Thornton, Tesla, and Jasper; the first was in Boston, then Arlington, and last month they met in London. He's also had at least two separate meetings with Jasper. I'm sure there have been frequent phone communications as well, but nothing on the Internet. They don't seem to trust the Internet."

"Probably took the hint from a couple of CEOs doing time in federal penitentiaries," Rick interjected.

Matty ignored Rick's comment and continued, "Before each meeting, Jimmy produces a set of notes for each man; he puts 'em in a file folder sealed with silver tape, the sticky kind of tape that can't be peeled back. He types the notes up himself and shreds the files after the meetings. At the Boston meeting, as everyone arrived, Jimmy passed out the folders. But, for the Arlington meeting, Jimmy had me take the folders from Doctor D's downtown office to the DSC building where the meeting was being held; not Doctor D's file though, Jimmy held on to that. Building 'C' in Arlington has a separate lobby, a lobby with a private entrance for VIPs and diplomats. I was seated in that lobby waiting for the three men and Doctor D to arrive; there was no one else in the room, so I decided to try to carefully fold back the corner of the black file cover on one of the reports to see if I could read any of the contents. I couldn't see much, but what I was able to read at the top of a page made the hair on my neck stand out straight. You ever hear of a radiological dispersal device, an RDD?"

"A dirty bomb," Rick replied.

Matty nodded. "You got it, a dirty bomb. I had a few minutes more with the file before the general arrived, then the two others came right after him. In the short time I had to snoop, and the tiny amount of print I could see, nothing else caught my attention. The next day when I told Taylor about the RDD, he didn't seem concerned. I thought it a bit odd that he—"

"Not really," Rick interrupted. "DSC frequently gets involved assisting government agencies develop contingency plans, what-if scenarios, that sort of thing; could have been part of a study for handling a dirty bomb."

Matty frowned. "It wasn't a study."

Rick started to speak, but Matty held up her hand. "There's more, lots more. Week before last at the meeting in the DSC London offices, I had the opportunity to read a lot more of the current file and to scan a second report as well. After the regular meeting, the general and Tesla left to catch a plane, but Doctor D and Jasper stayed behind. Jasper asked Jimmy to go down to the cellar and get a bottle of wine, then went back into the library with Doctor D and closed the door. Jimmy took the elevator to the cellar, but he left the now unsealed file folders on the desk, the desk where I was sitting! I guessed I would have at least four or five minutes before Jimmy realized he'd left the folders unguarded, and I knew that I'd either hear his footsteps on the creaky, old wooden stairs or the elevator bell when the elevator reached my floor. So, I dove into the unsealed files. This is what I found out: they've finished building the bomb and they've secured the radioactive materials they need; both should be on the way to the target soon."

"What target, where?" Cynthia asked.

"I don't know! I never found out! You gotta understand I was scared stiff that Jimmy would sneak up on me, or that Doctor D or Jasper would come out of the library and catch me reading. I read as much as I dared in the few minutes I thought I had, and then carefully closed the files and went to the ladies' room. I figured that if I was gone when Jimmy arrived and he found the files undisturbed, he'd likely assume that I hadn't noticed them."

Rick shook his head. "That's *it*, that's *all* you found out?"

"Two more things," she said. "Understand, I was under pressure."

"Yeah, Ricky," Cyn chimed in. "Be nice."

"Sorry about the tone of voice," he replied. "I doubt I'd have had the nerve to do what you did."

Matty slid forward to the edge of the couch. "They're looking for a suicide bomber, a man to carry the RDD to the target, a big man, strong enough to carry the bomb."

"And? You said there were two things?"

She nodded. "November, they're going to explode the bomb in November, the first week of November."

"Election day!" Cyn exclaimed.

Rick frowned. "Unlikely, no high-profile federal elections this year." Rick slapped his forehead with the palm of his hand. "Good God! Mustafa! Mustafa, our doorman, told me he's going on the Hajj this year, first week of November!"

"Mecca, the Hajj to Mecca?" Cynthia whispered.

Rick slowly nodded. "Mecca, Islam's holiest site. All Muslims, if they have the money, are required to make the Hajj, the pilgrimage to Mecca, at least once in their lives."

Matty's pale-blue eyes seemed to have doubled in size. "A dirty bomb would make the place radioactive, Muslims wouldn't be able make the Hajj; no one could survive the radioactivity."

"At least for four or five years," Rick added.

"Revenge," Matty exclaimed, "for nine-eleven?"

"Don't think so," Cyn said. "Father doesn't do revenge, says it uses up too much of his creative energy. . . Maybe we're jumping to conclusions too fast; lots of other events around the world take place during the first week of November besides elections and the Hajj."

"No, I think we nailed this one," Rick replied.

Rick turned toward Matty. "Any more meetings before November?"

"One more, I haven't been told where or when; not even sure I'll be required to attend. In any case, there's little chance I'd get another opportunity to look at the files; Jimmy's security lapse in London was a fluke."

"Cyn, maybe it's time for you to have a talk with your father, do a little fishing; now, if we can just figure out what bait to use to draw him out, and without blowing Matty's cover."

Cynthia frowned. "Screw the fishing, a dirty bomb would kill and sicken a lot of innocent souls. It's time for a confrontation with dear old Dad, the heart-to-heart I've avoided for the last thirty years." She held out her empty glass toward Matty. "I think I'll have some more wine, please."

SEVENTEEN

It seemed like everyone in Lisson Grove had crowded into the small cemetery. The townspeople, along with a handful of curious strangers, stood behind the stones and markers, all the way from the church entrance down the path to the four-foot-high wrought-iron fence that marked the border where the cracked sidewalk ended and the mowed weeds that passed for grass began. The town maintenance crew had hurriedly painted the fence a shiny black. The mayor was positioned inside the gate soberly shaking hands or nodding to each person who entered. One deputy sheriff directed traffic while another stood inside the cemetery gate, discreetly keeping the media and the TV cameras on the other side of the fence. Because of the mistaken identity connection with the famous Moesha Trabar, news of the attack at the Eden Hotel and Mu's killing had been broadcast around the world. The citizens of Lisson Grove were dazed and confused; the terrorists, whose atrocities appeared nightly on their TV screens, had murdered one of their own. Overnight the TV images had become personal, and the previously far-away video world beyond Lisson Grove, real and dangerous.

The Reverend Tony Jiggs, dressed in a new dark suit and the starched clerical collar he rarely wore during the summer months, stood at the head of the open grave. Ina, Rosa, and Rusty, his left arm in a sling, were to the Reverend's right; Ina clasped Rusty's free hand while Rosa supportively had an arm around his waist. Leo, head downturned, stood next to Rosa. On the opposite side of the open grave were Rusty's brother and sister, their spouses and four children, along with Patsy and two more of Muriel Samadi's foster children. Gladys and a half dozen of Mu's school lunchroom coworkers, along with Charley Hocter and Mrs. Kovacs, completed the graveside group. It was Saturday, so most of the elementary-school teachers and many of the students had come to mourn their lunch lady.

Mu's grave was next to Carol-Lee's; when Mu's headstone was erected, their two markers would be only a few feet apart. There was a space reserved for one more tombstone next to Mu.

It was a warm, sun-filled morning, a morning that would become a sticky, South Florida summer afternoon. Mockingbirds sang from the live oaks that surrounded the property, while a red-tailed hawk sailed overhead, shrilly protesting the mass invasion of her territory.

The Reverend Jiggs nodded, and his wife, Megan, led the children's choir in the first of two songs they would perform that day.

"Jesus loves me, this I know—" Their sweet voices stilled the crowd. Many of the mourners softly joined in the final chorus: "Yes, Jesus loves me, yes, Jesus loves me; yes, Jesus loves me, the Bible tells me so."

"We are gathered here together to celebrate a life," the preacher began, "a beautiful life, tragically cut short by the sword of hatred and intolerance."

* * *

Rusty desperately needed to get away from people, away from the endless condolences and testimonials to Mu's caring, gentle soul. And yet, he was terrified of being left alone in the home he and Mu had shared for nearly thirty years; alone with the photos of the children, photos of Mu at their twenty-fifth anniversary party in Ali's bar; alone with her painting of deer in a snowy pine forest, the painting Mu painstakingly crafted from the paint-by-numbers kit that Rusty had given her on their first Christmas together, the painting Mu had proudly hung over the living-room couch; alone with her clothing and a hairbrush with strands of her dark hair tangled in the bristles; alone at night with her sweet scent lingering on the bed pillow; alone.

Rosa and Leo begged Rusty to stay on with them for another week, just until his arm was strong enough for him to drive, but Rusty refused. He knew that he and Tater had to go home; go home and begin the painful process of building a new life, an empty life, a life without Mu.

That first night at home Rusty slept in the guest room with Tater curled in a tight ball between his legs.

Ina called the next morning to let him know she had arrived home safely. Rusty was excited to talk with her; although they had known each other for only a few months, their shared tragedy had permanently cemented their relationship. Ina promised to call back in the afternoon from the rehabilitation center so that Rusty could talk with Robbie. Rusty was glad that Robbie had Ina to care for him. The doctors were pleased with Robbie's progress. His left shoulder was now held together with metal rods and screws but the prognosis was positive, he'd regain nearly full use of his arm. One doctor suggested that tennis and golf might be out of the question; but then, Robbie didn't play tennis or golf.

Rusty hadn't had his medication in days and his GERD was flaring up, the fire from his stomach reaching up into his throat. He hesitantly opened the master-bedroom door and walked to the medicine cabinet without looking in the direction of Mu's dresser and the collection of framed photos. The guest-room bed was uncomfortable for Rusty's large body; maybe tomorrow night he'd return to their bedroom and their large bed, but not tonight, not just yet.

In the kitchen, Rusty filled his insulated tumbler with iced tea and washed down the blue capsule. He refilled the mug, went out to the screened porch and sat in the wooden-slat resort chair that Mu had given him on his birthday several years ago. He stared, uncomprehendingly, at the backyard while he finished the iced tea. Leo had cut the grass while they were in New York, but Rusty saw that it would need to be done again in a day or two.

That's the way his life with Mu had been; doing the same simple things over and again. It had been a pleasant enough life.

Outside the screen, Tater was repeatedly chasing, catching, and then releasing a gecko that had strayed from the safety of the latticework around the bottom of the porch.

Rusty closed his eyes and visualized Mu sitting in the padded rocker by his side. She was reading the paper and commenting on the local news for his benefit.

The doorbell rang; it was actually more a buzz than a ring. Rusty was surprised, no one used the front door; he couldn't remember the last time it was opened.

"Come around the back," he called through the open front window. "The door's stuck."

"Okay," a male voice replied.

Strangers; more news people, Rusty thought.

Tater was pawing the screen door, there was no sign of the gecko; it had either escaped or been eaten. Rusty held the door open for the cat.

Two men in dark suits turned the corner and strode toward the porch.

"Mister Samadi?" the smaller man in front asked.

"If you're reporters, I don't have nothin' more to say."

The man held up an open leather case with a gold badge on one side and picture ID on the other. "FBI," he said, "not reporters. You're Rustam Samadi?"

Rusty nodded. "Rusty," he said.

"Special Agent Carlson," the first man said.

The taller man with a shaved head held up his credentials. "Agent Biggs."

"Can I see your badge again?" Rusty asked Agent Carlson.

The ID clearly stated Federal Bureau of Investigation, and the picture looked like the man holding the leather case. "Okay, looks real," Rusty said. "What can I do for you?"

"Mister Samadi, we'd like to talk with you about the events in

New York eight days ago, your wife's murder."

Eight days, Rusty thought, *has it been that long*?

"I already talked with the police in New York; told them everything I could remember."

"Agent Biggs and I apologize for barging in on you like this. We appreciate that this is a difficult time for you and offer our condolences for your loss. But, some questions need to be asked, things the local police wouldn't have covered. Please, can we come in; this won't take too much of your time."

Rusty held the screen door open. He pointed to the round table and four plastic chairs in the corner. "Have a seat. You want some iced tea?"

The two agents declined.

"Let me get myself some more tea and a towel to wipe off those chairs; things get dusty out here this time of year."

Rusty poured the tea and took a damp kitchen towel to the porch. He quickly wiped down two of the chairs and sat in a third.

"Mind if we take off our jackets?" Agent Biggs asked. "Gets uncomfortable fast once you step out of the A/C in the car. Guess you get used to the heat when you live here?"

Rusty nodded, and the men folded their suit coats over the back of the fourth chair. Their long-sleeved white shirts were already damp.

"What's this all about?" Rusty asked. Tater sat on Mu's rocker staring at the men as if he, too, wanted to know the purpose of their visit.

Agent Carlson shuffled around in the plastic chair. "To come straight to the point, Mister Samadi, we're here to ask for your assistance, your help in bringing to justice those responsible for killing your wife and injuring yourself and your son."

Rusty placed his large hands on the table and leaned forward. "Like I already said, I told the New York police everything I know."

Agent Carlson shook his head. "Let me try again. We're not asking about what you can remember, Mister Samadi, we're asking for your assistance."

Rusty was confused. "I don't understand," he replied.

"First, we'd like to verify some information with you, and then we'll discuss the specific help we have in mind. Will that be acceptable to you, Mister Samadi?"

Agent Biggs extracted a beige file folder from his leather case. "We've gathered a considerable amount of information about you, Mister Samadi, and we'd like to make sure that everything we have is accurate."

Rusty shrugged. "Why do ya want to know about me? My wife's the one they killed. It was a case of mistaken identity, that's what the police said, the TV news, too."

"Please, Mister Samadi, this will just take a few minutes and then we can discuss the details of the assistance we're requesting."

Rusty sighed. "Okay, you *are* the FBI; I guess that gives you the right to do things your way. Ask away."

Agent Biggs took a set of printed sheets from the file folder. "We have a considerable amount of information to go over, Mister Samadi. Rather than have you answer yes or no to the accuracy of each detail, I'd suggest that I read and you stop me if there's anything incorrect or anything requiring explanation. Do you agree?"

"Whatever you say," Rusty replied.

Agent Biggs began. "You are Rustam Kas Samadi; you are fifty-seven years old and were born in Lisson Grove, Baron County, Florida; your parents are deceased, your father's name was Farid Samadi, your mother's Saman Samadi, née Moradi; your parents were born in Iran; your father was a CIA operative and was extracted from Iran before the fall of the former government and relocated here to Lisson Grove."

Rusty frowned. "CIA operative, you're positive?"

"Positive," Biggs replied. "He was a senior official in an Iranian ministry and collected data on electricity usage. Several letters of commendation are in his CIA file. He received a significant lump-sum payment and a small pension when he was relocated. He never told you?"

Rusty shook his head. "Never."

Biggs resumed. "Elder brother, Ali Samadi was born in Iran, younger sister, Shahana McKenna, born in Lisson Grove. Brother and sister both live in Key West; brother owns a restaurant and bar, sister is a housewife and manages a souvenir shop. Okay so far?"

Rusty nodded. "CIA; you're sure? My father was always a quiet, timid sort a guy."

"I guess he wasn't always so timid," Carlson said with a trace of a grin.

Agent Biggs continued reading the record of Rusty's life. Rusty was overwhelmed with the extent of detailed information the FBI had collected: school records, military and employment history, Mu's background and relatives, a history of their foster children. After reciting facts and figures for nearly fifteen minutes, Agent Biggs turned to questions.

"Mister Samadi, have you ever traveled outside of the United States, maybe to Canada or Mexico?"

"Only travel I ever done was with the army and in the U.S.: Jersey, Virginia, South Carolina, that's it."

"Have you ever had or applied for a passport?"

Rusty shook his head. "Nope."

"Do you consider yourself to be an adherent to the Muslim faith?"

"My parents was Muslims but didn't practice their religion much after they moved here. Father taught Ali an me ta read from the Koran and another book about Islam, but he stopped his teaching when I was eight or nine. Ali owns a bar and Shanna's married to an Irishman, what's that tell you? I'm not really anything. If you have to write down religion, put Christian, like Mu."

"Your wife was a Christian?" Biggs asked, although he already knew the answer.

"Mu was a Christian. She went to church most Sundays, and when the kids lived with us, she took 'em, too. I went along on Christmas and Easter; I like the singin', the music."

"You read and speak Farsi; isn't that right?"

"Not really, Father taught me and Ali some Farsi but that stopped when the religion lessons stopped. I think Father was plannin' on taking us back to Iran someday, but he changed his mind; don't remember the details, you'd have to ask Ali."

"But you can speak some Farsi?"

Rusty nodded. "A little; when I was stationed at Fort Lee there was this sergeant who spoke Farsi; I could understand him a lot of the time."

"Do you have any personal connections in Iran; family, friends?"

"I'm sure there's family, but no one I know. No relatives ever came to visit, no letters or Christmas cards either. . . All right guys, that's enough, no more questions, tell me why you're here."

Agent Biggs scribbled on the last sheet and then put the papers back into the file folder.

Agent Carlson shifted his plastic chair to face Rusty; Tater had grown bored with the conversation and was curled up, asleep on Mu's rocker. "Mister Samadi, an agency of the United States Government is planning a strategic military strike against fanatic Islamist terrorists, the same sort of terrorists who murdered your wife and shot your son and yourself. This is an important action that could destabilize these terrorists' ability to act for years. Your country needs your help to successfully carry out this mission."

Rusty started to ask the obvious question—*why me?*—but

Carlson held up his hand before Rusty could speak.

"Mister Samadi, you have some unique qualifications that are critical to the success of this mission. You are of Iranian descent and can pass as an Iranian; you can speak some Farsi; you are a large, strong man; through your military service and the manner in which you've lived your life, you've demonstrated your loyalty to the United States; and, you have just cause to seek retribution on those who destroyed your family."

Rusty grinned. "I think you boys got the wrong guy; in the army I worked in the motor pool, fixed cars and trucks. Basic training was the closest I ever got to weapons or combat. Besides that, I'm fifty-seven, have GERT, and am gettin' a paunch; hardly the kind of guy you'd want for a critical mission."

Agent Carlson placed his palms flat on the table. "Actually, Rusty, you are a one-in-a-million, perfect fit for this mission. That's why we're here; your country needs your help."

* * *

Nicholas Donner was seated at his desk, hunched in front of the speakerphone. "Johnston and Doctor Weiss are waiting outside," he said, "they've just returned from Florida. Before I bring them in, tell me about the meeting; everyone still on board?"

Martin Jasper cleared his throat. "You're at the Cabin, on a secure line?"

"I am, but I'd suggest that we speak as if we're on an open connection."

"Right," Jasper replied. "I met with the assistant to the Custodian's representative last night; we drove around London's streets for a half-hour in one of their limos; they're terrified of leaks. They've agreed with the plans we put forward."

"Everything?"

"The target our man will replace is a large man, a wealthy industrialist being accompanied by his son. They'll stay at a high-end hotel, one that's frequented by Shia. The hotel's within walking distance. . . That's it."

"They're guaranteeing access?"

"They are, but with no explanation as to how."

Donner grinned. "Doesn't matter, we have the details on their security. Good work, Martin. Let's get Johnston and Weiss in; we're on a roll, just one more piece to the puzzle."

Donner pressed a button on the phone. Jimmy opened the door and the two men entered Doctor Donner's office. Donner stood, shook hands with the men, and motioned toward the leather couch in front of his desk. The men quickly took a seat. "My associate's on the speakerphone. Johnston and Doctor Weiss have joined us."

"Gentlemen," Martin Jasper offered in greeting.

"We're on a secure line," Doctor Donner said, "but I suggest that we speak like we're on an open connection."

Johnston and Weiss nodded.

"Johnston and the Doctor just got off the plane; they interviewed the subject this afternoon. I haven't heard their report yet so this will be a first. Doctor, we're all ears."

Doctor Weiss moved forward to the edge of the leather couch and spread his papers on the coffee table in front of him. "Can you hear me okay? I'm speaking at normal volume."

"Loud and clear," Jasper responded.

"Let me start with a summary," Doctor Weiss said. "The subject meets all of the physical characteristics specified. From his physique, I'd assume he's got the strength required."

"How about the injury?" Jasper asked.

"Nasty flesh wound with considerable blood loss; shooter used hollow-point ammo," Johnston responded. "New York physician said no damage to organs or bone. Subject should be back at work soon."

Doctor Weiss continued, "My informal assessment of intelligence is acceptable for our purposes; army induction tests indicated slightly below average, but that was thirty-four years ago. It would be a mistake to confuse his lack of goals and motivation with low intelligence. It appears that he was genuinely satisfied with his low-key life, at least until now. He's grieving very deeply for his wife but hasn't been able to release his pent-up feelings yet. I'd judge him to be a loyal American; nothing came up in our records search that would indicate emotional or family ties to his parents' homeland or religion, same for his brother and sister. His target language skills were once at a young child's conversational level, and at his age and intelligence, with moderate training, they could be restored to that level in a relatively short time. I specialize in making in-the-ballpark analysis from limited data and observation. My professional opinion is that the subject is a marginally intelligent, mentally healthy, well-adjusted, late middle-aged, unsophisticated, unmotivated, American couch potato in the making—"

"Sounds like our man," Donner jumped in.

Doctor Weiss looked toward Johnston. "There does seem to be a problem, though. He's not demonstrating signs of anger, or rage, or a desire to avenge his wife's death. He seemed more curious about the proposed mission than interested in—"

Johnston cut him off. "We need to feed his anger, get him stirred up. Now that we know a lot about him, I've got some ideas for lighting his fuse. I'll need cooperation and assistance from local government and law enforcement; can we make that happen?"

"South Florida, that right?" Donner asked.

Johnston nodded. "Lisson Grove, Baron County."

"Baron County, huh? Congressman from down that way's just dying to repay my kindness. Exactly what kind of local assistance will you need, Agent Carlson?"

EIGHTEEN

District Office of Representative Tomas T. Maderos was boldly painted on the storefront window in gold script, outlined in black. The paint was chipped, the gold fading to mustard-yellow from years of exposure to the intense subtropical sun. A handful of dead flies lay on the curling-at-the-edges linoleum floor beneath the plate-glass window. A row of brown file cabinets lined the side wall, and a battered oak desk, three oak side chairs, and an American flag in a floor stand completed the sparse furnishings. Congressman Maderos was chairman of the House Homeland Security Committee and a protégé of Nicholas Donner.

"Thanks for coming here to meet with me, Sheriff Kerns; I'm trying to keep a low profile in your community." Johnston had decided that it was too chancy to use his FBI credentials with a law officer. Except for Johnston's tipped-in photo, the credentials were real, but the sheriff's reputation as a smart, resourceful investigator made Johnston think that Kerns would verify his authenticity with the district FBI office, and discover that Special Agent Charles Colby Carlson had been dead for four months. Today, Johnston was Ralph Derkis, Physical Security Inspector, Office of the Attorney General, Department of Justice. The real, deskbound Ralph Derkis entered and exited his D.C. office building each day with an ID badge; it would take awhile before he noticed his seldom-used credentials had gone missing.

Representative Maderos' lone aide had gone to lunch and Johnston and Sheriff Kerns were alone in a small meeting room, at the rear of the Congressman's main office. They were seated on either side of a worn oak table whose top was covered with years of cigarette burns and round stain rings from cups, glasses, and bottles. Johnston guessed that most of the cups and bottles had held something stronger than coffee or Coke.

Sheriff Kerns held up the freshly printed card that Johnston had placed on the table along with his credentials. "Okay, Ralph, you got my curiosity up; what exactly does a Physical Security Inspector for the DOJ do for a livin'?"

Johnston returned Ralph's credentials to his jacket pocket. "Like most jobs, I do what my boss tells me to do and count the days 'til retirement."

The sheriff grinned. "Don't sound very exciting, Ralph. Tommy says that you're doin' something real important for the US of A and that I should help you out. So, Ralph from the Inspector General's Office, what can I do for you?"

"You know Rustam Samadi?"

"Hell yeah, everybody in South Florida knows about Rusty; don't ya watch TV? Rusty's wife got herself killed by some terrorists in New York City; it was all over the news."

"What I meant was do you personally know Rustam Samadi?"

Kerns pushed the old wooden chair back onto its rear legs. "Depends on what you mean by *know*. I know who he is; I know who most people are in this county. If you mean do I know him well, I don't. He's the garbage man. Big, quiet guy with a house just outside of town; keeps to himself, doesn't hang out in the local bars or get in fights. He and his wife used to go down to the Moose couple times a month for dinner; he's a member at the Legion as well, I've seen them there at the Saturday fish fry. His wife ran the lunchroom at the local elementary school for years. She was a very popular lady; whole town was genuinely broke up by her killing. That what you wanted to know?"

"That'll do. . . Sheriff, there was a lot more goin' down in New York when Mrs. Samadi got killed and Samadi and his son shot up; more than was reported on the news or in the papers. I'm not a high-enough pay-grade to know all the details and I couldn't tell you if I did, but there was more to it than either of us will ever know."

Sheriff Kerns pushed his chair up straight and placed his

palms down on the tabletop. "I don't believe that Rusty or his wife was involved with terrorists, they're just small-town folk; not like the screwed-up people in New York City or Washington."

"No one's claiming the Samadis were involved with terrorists. This guy Trabar was the target, maybe his daughter as well, that's for sure. Thing is, the intercepted Islamist chatter in New York is full of questions about Samadi; no one knows why. Some of the higher ups in Justice think that Samadi could be very useful in helping flush out the others in the terrorist cell that carried out the shooting in the hotel. The FBI's talked with Samadi, asked for his help; so far, he's refused. . . That's where you come in; help get Samadi to change his mind about cooperating."

The sheriff shifted his large body around in the wooden chair. "Already told you, I don't know Rusty that well; if he won't listen to the FBI, not much chance I could talk him into helping you."

Johnston grinned. "We don't need you to talk with Samadi, we need you to arrest him."

Sheriff Kerns frowned. "Arrest him, what for? Is it a federal offense now to refuse to help the government?"

"You'll have reasonable cause for the arrest. By the time you get back to your office, a not-so-sweet old lady, local resident, someone you'll recognize, will turn up to make a complaint—a complaint against Samadi; his helper, guy named Hocter; and a pawnshop owner called Zornig. You know 'em?"

The sheriff's frown grew deeper. "Hocter's a harmless, feeble-minded old guy, member of my church; Leo Zornig owns an antique business and a pawnshop, he's one of the most respected citizens in town. He's been the unofficial 'mayor' of the Hispanic community for years. None of these men are criminals; what's this all about?"

Johnston ignored the sheriff's question. "As you'll see from the complaint, the three men stole some jewelry and some antique books from the lady in question; then they tried to sell the jewels and books in Zornig's antique shop."

"I don't believe it; sounds like a trumped-up charge."

Johnston nodded. "You can believe it. The lady will offer you proof that she's the owner of the property; you'll find most of the jewelry and the books for sale at the antique store. I think it's likely that the men will admit to the theft."

"This smells like a setup. This how you federal guys operate?"

"Sheriff, we want you to arrest these three men, and then call a Dana Coyle at the County Prosecutors' Office; I'm sure you know Ms. Coyle?"

Sheriff Kerns nodded.

"Ms. Coyle'll take it from there. She'll suggest that you release the suspects on their own recognizance. Best if you handle this yourself; no reason this matter needs to show up in the local papers."

The sheriff shook his head in disgust. "I don't want any part of your sleazy deals; find someone else."

Johnston placed his cell phone on the table. "I'm sorry, Sheriff, but you don't get a vote. Let me get Congressman Maderos on the phone, he'll be able to help you understand."

It took only a few minutes to get the congressman on the line; he was obviously expecting the call.

"Yeah, Tommy, it's Butch Kerns; I'm in your office in Lisson Grove, with this bureaucrat from the Justice Department. He says I gotta arrest Leo Zornig and Rusty Samadi on some trumped-up charges."

The phone conversation took only a few minutes; the sheriff snapped the phone shut and returned it to Johnston. The lines on his forehead were twisted in puzzlement. "You win," he said. "Can't see how these old boys could get theirselves mixed up in a matter of national security."

"I don't want anyone to get hurt," Johnston said. "Least of all Samadi, he's already in his own private hell." He extended his hand to the sheriff. "Sorry about the strong-arm tactics."

Sheriff Kerns got the patrol car's A/C blowing at full speed before taking the cell phone from his shirt pocket. He dialed the number on the printed card that Johnston had given him.

The phone rang five times before the Donner Systems Corp employee answered. "Department of Justice, Mister Derkis' office," she said.

"This is Sheriff Joseph Kerns from Baron County, Florida; can I please speak with Mister Derkis?"

"I'm sorry, Sheriff, Mister Derkis is traveling and he won't be back in the office until Friday. Can I take a message or give you his cell number?"

"No, thank you, Ma'am, I'll try him again on Friday."

He closed the phone and returned it to his pocket along with the fake business card.

Johnston had stayed behind in the congressman's office and was on his cell phone; he had reassumed the identity of Special Agent Carlson. "There's nothing concrete, Mister Samadi, just your name turning up in wiretapped phone conversations; questions about your background and where you live. We pick up lots of terrorist chatter on the telephone network in the New York area. Dozens more out there like Osman Kassim. The ones we know about are angry young students, busboys, young professionals; they're just waiting for someone to point out a target and put a gun in their hand; just like Kassim."

"I don't believe this," Rusty replied. "They shot me an' Robbie and killed Mu, what more do they want?"

"We're not dealing with normal people here, hard to tell what they want. Maybe they think you're tight with Trabar?"

"Yeah, right, I never even met Trabar until after the shootings, when I woke up in the hospital."

"Like I said, the reason for the call is to let you know there's some outside interest in you. Since you've been home have you seen anyone tailing you, watching your home?"

"Look, Carlson, this is bullshit. I told you, just leave me alone. I'm a nobody; they're not interested in nobodies. Don't call again; if anything happens I'll call you, I got your number; you hear me?"

"I appreciate your feelings, Mister Samadi, but I urge you to call if you sense anything strange going on around you. If these guys are targeting you for whatever twisted reason, you'll know."

"Yeah, sure, gotcha."

* * *

Rusty was sitting in his big chair on the back porch, still irritated from the phone conversation with Agent Carlson, when a county sheriff's patrol car pulled up. The deputy sheriff rolled down the window and waved.

"Now what in hell you want, Michael; FBI send you to protect me?"

The tall, young deputy sheriff stepped from the car and walked the few steps to the screened porch. "FBI? What about the FBI, Mister Samadi?"

"Forget it, doesn't matter," Rusty replied.

The deputy shrugged. "How's your arm comin' along, Mister Samadi?"

"Just fine, Michael; doctor says I can go back to work on Monday."

"Julie and I are real sorry about Mrs. Samadi and Robbie. Everybody liked Mrs. Samadi, and Robbie an' me were friends at school; Julie knew Robbie, too, we double-dated a couple a times with Julie's sister."

"Thanks, Michael, but you didn't come by in a patrol car to tell me that; what's up?"

"Sheriff would like to talk to you; sent me over to give you a ride. Would it be okay for you to come into town now?"

"What for?"

"Don't have a clue, Mister Samadi, Sheriff just said he needed to talk with you and told me to come give you a ride."

Rusty stood and scowled. "Damned FBI," he swore.

Rusty's irritation was quickly turning to anger. "Look, Sheriff, this is all a freakin' cock-up. I think I know what happened."

Leo Zornig, Charley Hocter, and Rusty were seated around the small Formica-topped table in the Baron County Sheriff's office. The sheriff was perched backwards on a lightly padded, metal chair, his back to the door.

Rusty continued. "Mrs. Kellerman lives on Michigan Court, Michigan's the first street that got built in the Gardens. Back in those days, we used to take people's trash cans from the sides of their houses and put 'em back again after we dumped the trash in the truck. When they built all the other houses in the Gardens, the boss told me to pick up the trash only from the cans that were along the curbside. Carmen Anthony was the boss back then, he was runnin' for county commissioner, guess he wanted to say he was savin' people money."

The sheriff smiled. "Poor Carmen, always runnin' for something. Never did get elected."

Leo nodded. "Never got more than a handful of votes; don't think even his wife or kids voted for him."

Rusty frowned; he didn't want to talk about Carmen Anthony. "Town put a notice in the paper to tell the new people to put their cans out front. Everyone did except the folks on Michigan. Carmen had died, so I said 'what the hell,' an Charley and me kept takin' the cans from the sides of the houses along Michigan; still do."

"What's that got to do with the books and jewelry?" Sheriff Kerns asked.

"Didn't you say Mrs. Kellerman had the books and jewelry in plastic bags to take to her daughter in Port Charlotte?" Rusty replied.

The sheriff nodded. "Said she put the bags on the backseat of her car."

"Well, see, she has this three-foot-high brick wall by the house that hides her cans, and she parks her old station wagon right next to the wall. She musta put the bags down on the wall meaning to put them in the car. Charley probably figured they was goin' out with the trash can and brought them to the truck along with the can. When their can's full up, people put their extra stuff out in plastic bags."

The sheriff frowned. "She said the bags was on the backseat of her car."

Leo turned to Charley. "Can you remember if you picked up those bags of books and stuff from the wall."

Charley smiled; he was pleased to be included in the conversation. "There was six books; real nice ones and there was a mess a shiny necklaces and stuff, I don't know how many there was, I left 'em in the bag and didn't count 'em."

"Were the bags of books and jewelry on top of the brick wall or were they in the car?" the sheriff asked.

"Six books and a mess of necklaces an' stuff, in the bags."

"No use askin' about the wall," Rusty said. "Charley only remembers numbers; right, Charley?

"There was six books, I remember; good ones, Leo's sellin' 'em for ten apiece."

The sheriff shook his head. "Charley, were the bags on the brick wall or in the car? Think for a minute."

Charley followed the sheriff's instructions and waited, his hand on his chin, for the wall clock to click off sixty seconds before answering. "There was six books, nice ones, and a mess a jewelry."

Leo had had enough; he smacked his fist on the tabletop.

"Butch, this is damn crazy. We been salvaging stuff from the trash for years. We split the profits three ways, Charley gives his share to Mrs. Kovacs who puts it in the poor box at church, Mu used Rusty's money to help out her foster kids and some of the poor kids at the school, and my share goes into uniforms and equipment for the Little League. You know damn well that none of us are thieves or crooks." Leo's blood pressure was rising and his face had turned bright red. "And you know for a fact that I've never been accused of dealing in stolen property; not at the pawnshop or the business, not one time in twenty-seven years."

The sheriff stood. "Calm down, Leo, 'for you have a stroke; course you're not thieves. This is obviously a misunderstanding; Rusty's idea about the bags on the wall is most likely what happened. Mrs. Kellerman is goin' on eighty and probably doesn't remember as well as she used to. Thing is, when someone files a formal complaint, I gotta investigate, take it serious. Talked with Dana over at the prosecutor's office this morning; here's what she wants to do. First, you bring me Mrs. Kellerman's property from the shop, plus any money you made on the stuff you already sold, agreed?"

Leo nodded. "Don't think we sold any of it, least not as of a day or two ago."

"Dana and I'll take the property to Mrs. Kellerman and explain that there's no legal basis for prosecution. Dana says she doesn't want any of this to show up in the papers, so, she wants you two boys to take a week off, stay out of sight." He pointed to Rusty and Charley. "She's arranged for some guys from the county road maintenance crew to fill in for you for a week."

Rusty aggressively shook his head. "Not a good idea; them boys from the county don't know their ass from a hole in the ground, they'll miss collections, have the folks all callin' in, complaining. 'Sides that, they'll screw up the truck, it's runnin' on borrowed time as it is."

The sheriff gave Rusty a hard stare. "Let's just say you're not sufficiently recovered from your injury to go back to work yet. You don't get to choose; you and Charley take a week off or I lock the three of you up, right now. You got that?"

Leo patted Rusty's good shoulder. "It's only a week; you could use another week to recover."

Rusty looked down at the table. "This stinks," he muttered.

NINETEEN

It was five-forty-five in the morning when the phone rang. Rusty and Tater had been awake, up, and dressed for over an hour.

"Rusty, it's Jeannie Kovacs. I need your help, Charley's sittin' outside on the steps, he won't come in the house and it's startin' to rain; say's he's gotta wait for Leo to go to work."

"You told him we was on vacation?"

"I did, I told him exactly what you told me to say. He just looked down the street and said you was on vacation but Leo was comin' by real soon. Gave him an umbrella, but he wouldn't use it. I'm afraid he'll catch his death outside in the rain."

"Okay, Jeannie, I'll be right over. Maybe you could put a coat around him?"

"I'll try, if he'll let me," she replied, and hung up.

The sky was dark and threatening when Rusty pulled into Mrs. Kovacs' drive, but the rain was still only a hard drizzle. Charley was sitting on the bottom step, an old raincoat wrapped around his shoulders, an unopened umbrella by his side.

As soon as he saw the truck Charley quickly folded the coat and placed it and the black umbrella inside the door. He pulled the collar of his orange coveralls over the back of his neck and trotted to the pickup.

"Rainin', Rusty," was all he said as he pulled the door closed.

"You didn't remember what I told you, you and me are on vacation this week, we don't have to go to work."

"Yeah, I remembered what you said 'bout vacation, that means Leo will be drivin', but he didn't come pick me up; I was waitin' on the steps."

"No, Charley, you're on vacation, too, not just me; you don't have to go to work."

Charley was clearly puzzled. "But Leo can't drive and dump

the cans, too; it'd take too long with just one person."

"There's two guys from the county takin' over from us, we're on vacation, you and me, both of us."

"I don't wanna be on vacation, I don't want some guys taken' over, I wanna go to work, like always."

"No, Charley, we have to be on vacation this week, Sheriff said that he has to fix up things about the books and jewelry you took from the wall outside Mrs. Kellerman's house before we can go back to work."

"Yeah, six books and—"

Rusty interrupted, he was losing patience. "Damn it, Charley, Sheriff thinks we stole them books and we can't go back to work 'til next week, that's our punishment."

"Leo's sellin' them books for ten apiece."

Rusty's grief, pain, and loneliness exploded; he lost control of his emotions, he was angry, hurt, and scared all at once. "Get back in the house, Charley; you're not goin' to work anymore—"

"But Rusty, I—"

"Get out of the truck, Charley; it's all your fault you friggin' loony, you screwed up an' now me and Leo gotta pay for what you done! Get out of this truck!"

Charley stumbled from the pickup and stood by the side of the drive while Rusty spun wheels in reverse on the wet pavement, then shot down the road.

Charley stared after the receding pickup. "I'm sorry, Rusty, I won't do bad things no more, I promise." The first thunderclap resounded overhead as the rain started to fall in sheets.

* * *

"Rusty, it's Jeannie Kovacs again. I'm real sorry to bother you but Charley's locked hisself in his room, he won't come out an' he won't talk to me. I was gonna call the police, but thought it would be better to call you. . . Do ya think I should call the police? After you left, he just stood out there on the lawn in the pourin' rain. I got the umbrella and brought him in; told him to get out of the wet clothes and take a hot shower. He went into his room, but I never heard the shower run. He was talkin' real strange after he came in, said he'd done bad things and couldn't go to work no more."

"Damn, damn," Rusty swore. "Sorry about the French, Jeannie; I'll be right over. Try to keep talkin' to him 'til I get there."

Rusty grabbed the pickup keys and his baseball cap but didn't bother with a jacket. He ran from the lanai through the hard rain to the truck. Tater started to follow and stuck his head through the cat door, but when he saw the heavy rain, decided that it wasn't going to be an outdoor morning, and returned to his bed.

* * *

"Charley, Charley, open up," Rusty called, for the third time. "This lock got a key?" he asked Mrs. Kovacs.

"Somewhere around, I'll go check in my desk drawer."

"Look, Jeannie, I gotta break in this door; don't worry, I'll pay to get it fixed."

"Just do it," she replied.

Rusty was a big man, but it took several shoulder thrusts on the old oak door before the lock yielded to his weight and the door flew open, crashing against the wall.

"Charley!" Mrs. Kovacs screamed!

Charley's body was suspended in midair, swinging slowly, pendulum-like, from the ceiling fixture. He'd removed the white cord from the phone in the lounge, threaded it through the top link in the chain that supported the lighting fixture, wrapped the cord around his neck, and stepped off a desk chair and into oblivion.

Rusty burst into the room and grabbed Charley's torso,

pushing his body upward to take the pressure off the coiled cord around Charley's neck. "Get a knife and cut him down!" he shouted.

"Holy Mother, please protect this gentle soul!" Mrs. Kovacs mouthed as she ran to the kitchen.

Charley's body was cold in Rusty's muscular arms. Charley's town-issued, orange jumpsuit was still dripping and a large puddle had formed on the floor below his body. Rusty knew that Charley wouldn't be going to work again.

Mrs. Kovacs ran from the kitchen, hastily climbed on the desk chair, and cut through the phone cord. Rusty carefully lowered Charley's body to the floor, away from the puddle of water—his face was contorted, his eyeballs were protruding from their sockets, and his tongue, a sickly blue, hung limply from a corner of his similarly blue lips. Rusty fell to his knees next to the body and began to sob uncontrollably. Tears flowed down his cheeks and fell on Charley's waterlogged jumpsuit. He looked up to Mrs. Kovacs. "What have I done?" he wailed. "My God, what have I done?"

NINETEEN

Cynthia Donner Cappa was nervous and rhythmically drummed her fingers on the leather upholstery of the black Lincoln sedan. Although she wasn't paying much attention to Tilman's nonstop conversation, she welcomed the patter as an alternative to silence and injected the monologue with an occasional "Okay," "I see," or "That's interesting." Tilman had been Nicholas Donner's personal driver for years, but Cynthia had never before been alone in the backseat while Tilman sat behind the wheel. They cruised through the Maryland countryside, past the manicured horse farms, neat rural villages, and newer McMansions, nestled in the green hills and trees of midsummer.

"Just up ahead, Miss Cynthia, past the church; are you remembering any of this yet?"

Cyn shook her head. "I haven't been to the Cabin since mother was alive, not since I was nineteen or twenty. She and I and Dilly, mother's companion, would spend weekends here when there was something special going on in town, like balls or state dinners. Mother disliked staying in hotels, especially hotels in D.C. Did you get to meet Dilly? She was with Mother right up until the end."

"No, I'm afraid that I didn't have that pleasure; I met your mother only once, and that was in Boston, weeks before her heart attack. I vividly remember her; she was a fine lady, not many like her anymore."

Cyn smiled. "You would have liked Dilly, she was just like Katharine Hepburn in her older years; same infectious smile, same accent. Like Mother, Dilly came from a wealthy Boston family, they met at school. Somewhere along the way, Dilly's family went broke and her husband left her. That was when Dilly moved in with us; I always thought of her as Mother's sister, they were devoted to each other. Funny, I haven't thought of Dilly for years; guess it's coming to the Cabin that's bringing back the memory."

"Here we are," Tilman said, as he navigated down a twisting gravel road, over a stone bridge, through flowering trees and alongside well-tended lawns. "Do you remember now?"

"Mmm, yes; the Cabin's exactly the same, not changed at all."

"Well, except for the helicopter pad in the rear and all of the satellite dishes and electronics in the sheds; house is still the same."

As Tilman pulled the Lincoln to the entrance, Jimmy emerged from the front door. He was dressed in khaki trousers and a bright blue golf shirt. He strode up to the sedan with a big smile on his face and opened the door. "Cynthia, what a pleasure to see your lovely face once again."

Cyn stepped from the car; ignoring Jimmy's outstretched hand, she hugged him and kissed him lightly on the cheek. "James, you are immortal; you never change."

He smiled. "A little less hair and thicker around the middle, other than that, I'm doing pretty well."

"And Father?" she asked. "Haven't seen him since April; his birthday party."

"All things considered, Doctor D is in good health. A bit more ornery, but that goes with the arthritis and aging. Doctor gives him shots every few weeks; he says that keeps the stiffness and discomfort in check. If I make it to seventy-four, I hope I'm in as good shape as he is. Come on in, he's been pacing around his office waiting for you all morning. We've ordered in a special catered lunch; you will stay for lunch, won't you?"

She nodded. "Don't have to be back in town until the evening. I'm all yours."

Cyn took Jimmy's arm and they turned toward the house. Although "the Cabin," had begun life as an actual log cabin, it was no longer an appropriate name for the sprawling, single-story, white-painted brick structure that extended far beyond the footprint of the original nineteenth-century cabin.

"Sally's here?" Cyn asked.

Jimmy opened the large oak door. "Sally hasn't visited the Cabin in months; she's tied up with her projects at the university. Seems like your father's spending less time at the house as well and more time here. Sally calls him every couple of days."

Cyn shrugged. "Sally's been in her own world for a while now. . . How lovely!" Cyn enthused, as she stepped into the flower-filled entryway.

"We had the place completely redecorated year before last, hired a professional designer, but in the end I did most of the work myself; designer's concept of a masculine refuge was a bit too stark."

Cyn had never been entirely sure of Jimmy's sexual orientation. He'd been married as a young man and allegedly had two children with his now vanished wife. Cyn had never seen a picture of, or met, either child. When social events required a partner, Jimmy always showed up with the same woman, a plain, skinny, obviously intelligent woman he called Charity, a career officer at the State Department. Between events, Charity seldom appeared in Jimmy's life; it was as if she were an accessory he kept in a closet, wheeling her out when necessary for the required occasion.

Cyn was feeling devilish, and as they walked down the hallway she asked, "How's your friend Charity, I enjoyed talking with her at Father's birthday party."

"Charity is completely overwhelmed," Jimmy said, shaking his head. "She's on the North Africa desk and, with all the revolutions, is inundated, working long hours. If we're lucky, we get an evening together on the weekend, that's about it."

Cyn shook her head. "Too bad, give her my regards."

"I will, indeed," he replied with a grin, while knocking on the brilliant white enameled door to Doctor Donner's office.

Nicholas Donner opened the door and threw his long arms

around Cynthia's shoulders. "My darling girl, it's such a joy to have you here!"

Cyn was taken aback; her father was rarely openly affectionate. She stepped back from his embrace but held his large hands in hers. "I'm so pleased you invited me to visit, Father; haven't been here in ages, brings back so many memories, memories of Mother and Dilly and when I was a girl."

Donner held on to one of Cyn's hands and turned back into his office. "Come in, come in, we have so much to talk about, haven't we?"

"Yes, I guess we do, it's been a while."

"Shall I set up lunch for one o'clock, or do you want to call me when you're ready?" Jimmy asked Dr. Donner.

"You'll stay for lunch; you're not in a hurry?"

"I'd love to have lunch." She winked at Jimmy. "And a nice bottle of white Burgundy?"

"We can do that," Jimmy said and started to close the office door.

"I'll buzz when we're ready for lunch," Donner called.

"Let me look at you." He stroked her long dark hair. "You look just like your mother; same playful smile and childlike dimples. She really was a beauty, you know; you do remember?"

"Of course, Father; you know I was nearly twenty when she died. I clearly remember her face on the last day we were together. We went shopping for spring clothes and then had lunch at one of the Boston hotels, can't remember which one. We talked mostly about you, about how proud she was of you and how you'd grown the company. She didn't eat much, said she was tired. We cut our day short, and after lunch I put her in a cab for home—she smiled and waved goodbye. That was the last time I saw her alive, wearing a pink hat in the backseat of a cab."

Donner smiled. "She did like her hats. Please, sit down, here on the couch. Would you like coffee, or maybe tea?"

Cynthia placed her bag on the big desk and sat. "Not for me, thanks. You still drink a gallon of coffee a day?"

Donner grinned. "Yes and no: doctor made me switch to decaf for my blood pressure; Jimmy has this espresso decaf sent down from New York, even stronger than the real thing. Jimmy's got Taylor hooked on it, too."

Cyn shook her head. "Speaking of Taylor, you really are serious about stepping down, turning DSC over to Tay?"

"Taylor's been in charge for the last three years. He's grown sales more than ten percent year on year and PBT even more. The business is all technology now, things change too fast for my feeble old mind to track. Taylor's been training for this job since he left college, time to get out of his way."

"What'll you do; what's Sally think about having you home every day?"

"Sally's fine with my decision; she's up to her eyeballs with her research, don't expect she spends that much time at the house anymore, neither do I."

Cyn frowned. "You're both okay with that?"

"Cynthia, I'm seventy-four, Sally's seventy—relationships are different when you get to be our age. We're good friends and we support and help each other. Your mother will always be the love of my life, but Sally's my best friend. Sally's helped me understand life from a female perspective, important things: relationships, support, commitments, human needs and passions—things I'm not hardwired for, things that are outside my skill set. We've been a good team. I expect our relationship will survive until I croak. We just don't need the physical proximity we once did; sex isn't as big a draw when you get old."

Cyn blushed. "I didn't mean to pry. You know that I've always been very fond of Sally and grateful to her for taking care of you; not an easy job."

"And what about you? Taylor said you and Rick have decided to live here in the Watergate condo and that you're on leave from the museum; that right?"

"The condo's temporary; we're moving to a house, put a deposit on a three story in Georgetown last weekend. Nice place, reminds me of my house, mother's house, only smaller. I need to redecorate, former owners were Nigerian oil people; they left it in pretty rough shape. I'll have you over for dinner in a month or two, if you like."

"I'd like that very much. . . How about the museum?"

"I'm going to write my Gauguin book, the book I've been working on for ages, the book that refuses to write itself; that, and a few other projects I've lined up. I expect to be pretty busy for the next year or two."

"After that?"

"Like my father always told me, 'Don't fret over decisions until you're forced to make them.'"

"Your father must have been a procrastinator."

Cyn smiled. "It's all about Ricky, Father. I was forced to make a decision, and I chose Ricky. There was no contest. I'm a healthy, happy woman once again."

Donner patted Cyn's hand. "Always said that you were the smartest one in the family; that's why I chose you as the executor for my estate. Technically I think it's *executrix* in the case of a woman."

Cyn grinned and shook her head. "You're healthy as a horse; you won't need either for years."

"This horse is in his last race. They tell me that if I'm fortunate I'll have another ten months or so—then blindness followed by coma and death. Glioblastma multiforme, that's what the monster's called, we're on a first-name basis. I've been in and out of doctor's offices and hospitals for the last five months; no good, it's inoperable brain cancer."

It took several seconds for Cyn to absorb her father's casually delivered bombshell. She stared at him, taking stock of a tall, gawky, white-haired, hunched-over old man; a parent who had seldom been a part of her life; a near stranger whose genes, as if by a freak accident, coursed within her body. He was going to die and she knew that she would have to search deep within her psyche to find the emotions to care, to grieve. She realized that the conversation was on her side of the net and so she asked an obvious question. "You've told Sally and Taylor?"

Donner shook his head. "Only you, you're the first, although I did drop a few hints to Taylor last week."

"Tay got your message; the way he put it was that you seemed to be anticipating your death, maybe even enjoying the anticipation."

Doctor Donner laughed heartily. "Perhaps I am, perhaps I am. Few get the privilege of knowing in advance when they'll die. It's not information that's readily for sale. How much would you pay right now for the exact date and time of your death; a million, ten million? See what I mean? I've been given a gift, a free gift; not the exact date, but pretty close—a gift of time, of awareness, a chance to tidy up the crumbs and refuse of my existence; maybe even a chance for some do-overs. Don't misunderstand; I'm not talking about doing-over you and me. By any conventional standard I've been a miserable failure as a father."

Cyn felt a momentary reflex to disagree, to personally assume some of the blame for their bankrupt relationship. She resisted, she knew he was right, he'd been a failure; and yet, she saw the old man seated next to her on the leather couch through neutral eyes, not eyes of anger or resentment.

"Mother was a loving, nurturing woman; parenting came to her naturally, just like her warm smiles. She engulfed me and Tay in her tender affection; frankly, I didn't even realize you weren't a real part of my life, of our family circle of affection, until mother died. Then, of course, I had Ricky to fill up the emptiness in my heart that mother's death had left behind; he still does. It doesn't matter anymore, Father. You're wealthy, powerful, and an important cog in the machine that runs the world. You've lived your life as you wanted. I guess you've always been more a grandfather figure to me; someone to be respected and admired at a distance."

"You're not angry with me?" Donner placed his large hand over hers.

"Not at all, not even hurt or disappointed. I know you loved Mother; my childhood memories are full of images of you with Mother, you and Mother together."

Donner patted Cyn's hand. "I loved your mother with a passion that I think left little room for you and your brother in my crowded life. When she died, that passion flowed into my work rather than to my children; it's not an excuse, but I think I assumed that since you were both adults, you and Taylor would care for yourselves and each other and let me get on with what I thought was important for my company and my country. I'm truly sorry that I failed you as a father, but, in all honesty, I must admit that if I had the opportunity for a life do-over, I probably wouldn't change much."

"Rotten, egotistical, and self-centered, but totally honest; that's how I always described you to Ricky. After he got to know you he said that I was quite perceptive."

Donner smiled. "Yes, I think that's an accurate description; although I might quibble with the rotten bit."

Cyn shifted her position and as she moved to the edge of the couch, her black suede skirt squeaked on the leather. "So, you're sure this brain cancer isn't treatable?"

"Been to the best doctors money can buy; at the end of the day, they all offer variations on the same prognosis. When I first got the bad news, like most wealthy men, I rushed from one medical establishment to the next, assuming my money would entitle me to a cure. There's a clinic in Texas that thinks they can give me an additional year or more with surgery. My guy at Johns Hopkins, the one I trust the most, disagrees; he feels that any time I'd gain from surgery would be offset by an earlier downgrade of my mental capabilities; it's a losing proposition. The good news is that I should function near normal right up until the end, until the last month or so, and I won't need to be hospitalized until the blindness sets in."

"Are you really as calm about facing death as you're letting on?"

Donner stood, walked to the side table and poured a fresh cup of coffee. "Change your mind about coffee?" he asked. "Its decaf espresso, but we brew it like ordinary coffee."

Cyn shook her head.

Donner stooped to place the cup and saucer on the coffee table in front of the couch, but remained standing. "In an odd way I'm actually finding a perverse pleasure in the experience. It's as if I'm a third party watching the last days of Nicholas Donner; wondering what the old goat'll do next, speculating on whether he'll fall apart as he nears the end—it's like a laboratory experiment."

"Like playing God," Cyn nearly whispered.

"You could say that," Donner replied with a grin. "Like a minor god observing his creation. . . That's enough about me and glioblastma multiforme, at least for now. You'll take the job as my executrix?"

"If you want me to, of course I will; I'm surprised you didn't pick Taylor, he's got the business experience and legal background. Why me instead of Tay?"

"The distribution of my estate will need a woman's touch. Other than Milt Tobias, my attorney, and the doctors, you and Jimmy are the only ones who know about my condition. Of course, there was no way to keep the information from Jimmy. I'd like it to stay our secret for as long as possible; you agree?"

"Okay for now, but at some point I'll have to talk with Ricky; we don't keep things from each other anymore."

"I understand; but you'll let me know before you tell Rick? I'll have a talk with Sally and Taylor at the same time."

"I'll let you know before I say anything to Ricky."

Donner nodded and plopped his long body onto the couch. "The executrix task will be straightforward. You should see Tobias soon; I'll have him come down from Boston whenever you wish. Take a look at the will, at the monies I've set aside for you and Taylor, Sally and the twins. While I don't think any of you really need more than you already have, I've instructed Tobias to let you increase the amounts at your discretion, as much you wish. Jimmy and Kurt have been well provided for, Tilman too. Tobias will explain the details of what I'm doing with the bulk of the estate, but, in a nutshell, I'm distributing much of my shares among the employees and taking Donner Systems back to being a privately held company. Tobias and his firm, with Taylor's assistance, can manage the process; its complex—control of the company will stay within the Donner family while the rewards of DSC's continuing success will be passed to the employees, depending on their service and accomplishments. Once I tell Taylor about my imminent demise, he can meet with you and Tobias as well. As you mentioned, I already gave him an idea of what I've planned. You're okay with that?"

"Yes," was all that Cyn said.

"Good; just one other thing we need to discuss. For years, DSC has acted as an agent of the United States Government, taking on tasks our leaders were unable to execute through normal channels and—"

"Illegal projects?" Cyn interrupted.

"Actions that were impolitic, that might cause embarrassment to our government, and yes, sometimes actions that were important for our country's safety but not within the exact letter of existing legislation."

"Weasel words," Cyn interrupted again. "You mean like weapons for the contras?"

Donner looked his daughter square in the eyes. "Nations don't operate within the same rules as do private individuals. The United States has more enemies than friends. Great Presidents, such as Lincoln, FDR, and Reagan, for the good of the nation, had to sometimes operate outside of the normal channels of government, outside of the rules, even outside the law. DSC has been one of the resources our leaders have called on for assistance; a few times, they've called personally on me and I've responded." Cyn started to speak, but Donner waved his hand in the air. "Please, let me finish."

She slid back into the couch.

"Soon after my death, Tobias will give you an envelope that will contain the key and access instructions to a safe deposit box in Boston. In that box are files: transcripts, e-mails, telegrams, telexes, handwritten letters, and documents and, most important, my detailed diaries. If at any time leaks involving DSC or me should surface in the media—"

"You mean like Wikileaks?"

"Yes, Wikileaks or other media reports, stories that could cause harm or embarrassment to DSC; if such stories surface, you and Taylor are to open the box and retrieve the documents. It'll be obvious to the two of you how to use the information to protect DSC and yourselves. I've arranged for the deposit of documents to continue after my death so that you'll have protection from the future fallout of any current activities."

"Fallout, you mean like dirty bombs?"

Donner frowned but didn't hesitate with his reply. "I pray that you'll never need to open the box, but sometimes people in power will do anything to save their own skins; they'll betray and turn on whomever they see as a threat to their reputations. Not only will the documents in the box provide you with protection from falsehoods and lies, they'll also give you the tools to keep the jackals at bay and to better understand the actions of your rotten, self-centered, but honest father."

TWENTY

"Father Jerry said it's church law, people who kill theirselves can't be buried in a consecrated cemetery; nothin' he can do about church law. Father Jerry was real close to Charley, he's broke up pretty bad. Jeannie Kovacs really lit into him, told him she was thinkin' 'bout joining the 'Piscopals."

Rusty's lips turned up in a faint grin. "It don't really matter where he's buried, Rosa. If there's any kind of decent God, he's already welcomed Charley home."

Rosa lowered her head. "I guess you're right. Anyways, Pastor Jiggs did a good job with the service, considerin' he didn't know Charley that well."

Rusty nodded. "He did, didn't he. I liked the part where he said that Charley was a child in a man's body, and that in the old days Jesus told the guys in charge that they shouldn't stop the little children from hanging around with him, because Heaven belonged to the children. I can understand why Mu liked Jesus so much; he must have been a good guy."

Rosa dabbed at her eyes with the wad of tissues she'd held in her hand for the last few hours.

The sound of a car coming up the gravel driveway next to the house caught their attention.

"That'll be Leo," she said. "Sure you won't stay on for supper; it's only the two of us tonight?"

Rusty shook his head. "Gotta go feed Tater his dinner; just the two of us now as well. 'Sides, I got some more thinkin' to do. Like I told you before, Ali and Shanna want me to sell the house and come live in Key West. Ali and Marie have these apartments they rent out to the tourists; there's ten of 'em and a nice apartment for the manager. Marie manages the place, so she and Ali don't need the manager's apartment. They got a maid that cleans up, but Marie said she could really use my help as a handyman. You know, keep the plumbing and electrics workin', paint, fix roof leaks, and fix things around the bar as well. Marie says I can have the manager's apartment rent-free, and with the money I get from sellin' our house and the pension from the town, Ali thinks there'll be more than enough to take care of me and Tater for a long time. . . Ali's real good with money." Rusty lowered his head. "With Mu gone, and now Charley too, seems like I don't really need to be round here anymore."

Rosa patted Rusty's muscular arm. "You're really gonna do the early-retirement thing, huh?"

"Town's been after me ever since Mu died; they wanna bring in this contractor 'stead of puttin' up the cash for a new truck; over a hundred-seventy-thousand, that's what garbage haulers cost."

"I hope you're doin' the right thing. Anyways, just know that you'll have me and Leo to help you out if you decide to stay on; we're not goin' anywheres."

The corroded spring on the porch screen door squealed open and then slammed the door shut as Leo came into the kitchen. He was still dressed as he had been for Charley's funeral, in a short-sleeved white shirt and a dark-blue tie.

Rosa moved to Leo's side and kissed him on the cheek. "We was wonderin' where you got to."

Leo put his arm around Rosa's small shoulders and nodded toward Rusty. He stuck out his other hand. "How ya holdin' up, big fellow?"

Rusty shook his hand. "I'm okay; just gettin' ready to head out."

"I told him he should have some supper with us," Rosa said. "You tell him."

"Thanks, Rosa, but I gotta get home; Tater's used to gettin' his dinner when I get home from work, he'll be waitin'."

Leo pointed to the kitchen table. "Sit down for a few minutes, Rusty. I gotta tell you about the strange conversation I just had with the sheriff; won't take long."

Leo and Rusty sat across from each other while Rosa took a pitcher of lemonade from the refrigerator, gathered three tall plastic tumblers from the cupboard, and filled them with ice cubes.

Leo drummed his fingers on the table while he waited for Rosa to sit.

"How's Robbie comin' along?" Leo asked.

"Talked to him and Ina on the weekend; he's doin' real good. Ina said that she's takin' him home soon; he'll still have to go back to the rehabilitation center for regular treatments. Ina wanted to come down for Charley's service but I talked her out of it. Nice of her to ask, but she didn't really know Charley."

Leo smiled. "She's a keeper, that one."

"You want some taco chips or some pretzels?" Rosa asked.

The men declined; Rosa filled the three glasses and sat at the end of the table.

Leo placed his palms flat on the table. "I passed by the sheriff on the road near Ramos' produce stand, he waved me over and then we went to the diner for coffee. He was lookin' real serious and I was worried maybe one of the Herrera boys was in bad trouble again. That wasn't it; sheriff said Mrs. Kellerman came by his office late yesterday afternoon. He said she was real upset and told him she wanted to withdraw her complaint about the books and jewelry."

"Ha! Little late for that," Rosa complained.

"She said that her daughter put her up to it and that she was real sorry if her complaint had anything to do with Charley."

Rosa nodded. "I bet she was."

"Mrs. Kellerman told the sheriff that some guy with a funny accent called her daughter to ask if she knew that her mother's property was bein' sold in my antique store; valuable first-edition books on sale for next to nothin'. Said he thought maybe the books were stolen property. I told the sheriff the bit about first editions was nonsense; they were good-quality re-issues of classic novels, worth a little more than the ten bucks each I was charging."

"How'd he know the books belonged to Mrs. Kellerman?" Rosa interrupted.

"Book plates pasted in the front of the book with Mrs. Kellerman's late-husband's name and address. Daughter said the man told her that he was a book collector and that he would give Mrs. Kellerman one hundred bucks for each of the books. He told the daughter to go buy the books from the shop and then have her mother file a complaint with the sheriff. Said that she needed to file the complaint because he wouldn't buy stolen property, and if the books were stolen, this way he'd be sure that he wouldn't get in trouble with the law. He gave her a number to call after she got the books, said he'd come by with the six-hundred."

"He had a funny accent, you said; like a foreign one?" Rusty asked.

"Daughter said it was like in gangster films; maybe Boston or New York."

"Gangsters?" Rosa asked.

Leo shook his head. "Not gangsters; daughter said the man who called on the phone just sounded like a gangster, you know, like the way they talk on *The Sopranos*. So, the daughter went to the shop and bought the books for sixty bucks, got her mother to make the complaint, and then called the man. She got connected to a furniture rental store in Fort Myers who said they never heard of a man who buys books."

Rosa frowned. "How'd this man get Mrs. Kellerman's daughter's number?"

"Sheriff didn't say."

"Sounds like a bunch of bull to me," Rosa said.

Rusty pounded his big fist on the table. "FBI, damned FBI; they did this, they killed Charley!"

* * *

Rusty was angry, he was steering the pickup with his good arm and driving well over the speed limit. He needed to get home and call Agent Carlson, find out why in hell the FBI was playing games, why they had manufactured the story about the stolen books and called Mrs. Kellerman's daughter. There was no doubt in his mind that the FBI was behind Mrs. Kellerman's complaint and indirectly responsible for Charley's death.

Rusty knew his emotional, mixed-up explanation of his earlier meeting with the FBI agents had left Leo and Rosa thoroughly confused. He'd stop by and try to explain better in the morning, but first he had to talk to Carlson.

As he turned into his driveway, Rusty saw that someone had driven directly through Mu's flowerbed; the brilliant, red 'Crown-of-Thorns' she'd planted in a cluster where the drive turned toward the back porch had been broken and scattered onto the lawn. "Damn," he said aloud. "Damn FBI."

As he pulled the truck to a halt, Rusty saw the screen door crookedly hanging by the top hinge, banging in the light wind against the doorjamb. Someone had kicked in the screening on the bottom of the door as well. "What in hell?" he shouted. As Rusty climbed out of the truck, he saw the stain on the concrete-block wall; at about chest height, it was a large spatter of blood on the wall next to the kitchen door. It looked almost as if someone had purposely thrown a cup of blood against the wall. The bloodstain ran down the wall to a pool on the concrete floor below. Next to the pool of blood was a large black cat, his neck bent unnaturally backward. "Tater!" Rusty shouted as he fell to his knees and lifted Tater's limp, bloody body to his chest. "Bastards, bastards!" Rusty screamed. . . Then Rusty saw the writing on the white painted block wall above the bloodstain. Someone had repeatedly dipped their finger in Tater's blood and written two words: *ALLAHU AKBAR.*

"Bastards, Muslim bastards!" Rusty shouted. He stroked Tater's cold body and glared, transfixed, at the writing on the wall.

For some time, Rusty knelt on the concrete floor rocking Tater's mutilated corpse as if he were comforting a human baby. His mind raced, pounded inside his skull, pounded like river rapids—rapids boiling and frothing in a river of blood. He saw the terrorist drop the newspaper and soundlessly fire at Robbie and Mu, he saw Mu fall forward into a spreading pool of blood, Robbie's blood. He saw their contorted faces, watched Rosa scream, but heard nothing. He watched as Charley stepped off the chair; he saw Charley's head jerk back and his eyeballs protrude from his face, his body bobbing up and down from the beige telephone cord wrapped around his neck like a child's toy, a ball on an elastic tether. Over and over, the paralyzing images silently replayed until they abruptly stopped. It was if someone had pulled the plug on the movie projector running silently in Rusty's head. Rusty blinked, he stared down at the floor, the blood, the cat; he struggled to understand where he was, what had happened to him, to the world where he had recently lived. He started to sob, great gut-wrenching sobs shook his large torso; tears flowed down his chest to mix with the blood on his arms and hands.

It was still light when Rusty came out of the trancelike state that had temporarily transported his mind to another place, a place of silent suffering, a place in Hell. His legs and ankles were cramped and throbbing, his knees ached.

He gently laid Tater on the floor and holding onto the back of his wooden chair, painfully pulled himself upright. Rusty stooped and gathered Tater's lifeless body into his big hands. Hobbling, he carried Tater to the plastic table in the corner of the porch and placed him on yesterday's newspapers. Rusty inhaled deeply; he was exhausted, his entire body screamed with pain. "I gotta get out of here," he said aloud. As if in reply, he heard Mu speak to him, quietly calling, deep inside his head—he knew it was Mu's voice, there was no doubt. *"I'm waiting for you,"* she called; that was all she said. Rusty understood, he lowered his head to his chest, his course of action had been determined.

* * *

Just as the sun was about to set, Johnston pulled his rented SUV behind Rusty's pickup. He saw Rusty by the side of the house, digging a grave for the cat.

The sandy soil had easily yielded to Rusty's spade, and the opening in the earth was nearly three-feet deep. Tater's body, wrapped in a white pillowcase, lay next to the hole.

Johnston was unsure of Rusty's mental state and walked gingerly toward Rusty, and the hole.

Rusty stopped digging and leaned on the long-handled spade. "Never knew cats had so much blood in 'em."

Johnston shook his head. "Pretty cowardly; killing a pet."

"Bastards bashed his head up against the wall; smashed his skull, broke his neck."

"Anything else damaged?"

"Like I told you on the phone, they kicked in the screen door and killed my cat; that's it."

"Can I help?" Johnston asked.

"Nothin' much to do: no prayers, no speeches or flowers for a cat. Mu found him at the shelter after the first Tater died; she named him Tater-Two but we always just called him Tater. He was my good friend." Rusty stooped over, settled on one knee, and gently placed the pillowcase and Tater in the hole. He scooped up the damp earth with his big hands and covered the pillowcase, then stood and used the spade to fill the grave. "I'll cover it over with some rocks in the morning; keep the scavengers from diggin' him up." Rusty tamped the raw soil down, first with the spade and then with his boots. He wiped his soiled hands on his trousers and turned to Johnston. "Okay, Carlson, let me put this spade back in the shed and then we can go in and talk about who you need me to kill."

"It can wait until morning," Johnston replied.

Rusty wearily shook his head. "No, now; I need ta get out a here real soon. . .time to settle with the sons-a-bitches. . .write some bloody words on *their* wall."

Johnston followed Rusty to the shed, and then the two men turned and walked silently toward the house; Rusty never noticed the red and green branches of Mu's 'Crown of Thorns' twisted in the front bumper of Agent Carlson's SUV.

* * *

Doctor Donner read Johnston's text message for the second time. "Subject will assist—attitude adjusted." Donner didn't like cell phones and abhorred texting, but this particular message made him smile; Samadi was ready to cooperate.

Donner buzzed Jimmy at his desk.

"Yes sir," Jimmy answered.

"Call Jasper and tell him we have a go, an immediate go."

"Right away," Jimmy replied.

TWENTY-ONE

After surviving a twenty-year career of poisonous, clandestine projects, Martin Jasper knew the enemy well; it was hubris. Overestimating one's own intelligence or skills, believing the enemy less capable, celebrating stories of earlier cleverness, assuming that current success would continue unabated; hubris was a curse placed on the sanguine, and the trigger of a weapon pointed at the fool.

Martin Jasper always assumed that someone was purposefully watching his every move. The Sarasota rental property was both remote and secure, exactly what he wanted. It was owned by a paranoid Central American banker who stayed there only infrequently and lived his life in constant fear of him or his family being kidnapped for ransom. The owner had spared no expense to make the house secure. It could be accessed only by a long driveway that connected to an infrequently trafficked minor road. The property was surrounded by a high, steel picket fence and the perimeter and all access points to the house secured by a sophisticated movement-detection system. A rotating trio of guards and Doberman Pincers controlled the front gate. A Donner Systems executive, his wife and three children had vacationed at the rented house for a week before Doctor Weiss, Rusty and the others had taken over. As far as the renting realtor and locals knew, the executive and his family were still the only ones in residence.

Doctor Weiss, who Rusty knew as FBI Agent Biggs, was cooking scrambled eggs and sausages on the restaurant sized gas stove. Rusty hadn't strapped on the dummy bomb and harness he was required to wear four hours each day; it sat on a chair pulled up to the end of the long granite-topped island.

"When's the professor comin'?" Rusty asked.

"After breakfast; 'bout an hour. He says you're doin' good. You been listening to the *Farsi* recordings he left?"

"I listened once; couldn't figure out how to wind it back up to play again. I couldn't see the spools of tape inside, they must be real little."

"It's a digital recorder; no tapes. Bring it down after breakfast and I'll figure out how to rewind it and then show you."

"Haven't heard much Farsi since I was a kid; the voice on the recorder sounds a lot like Ali. Ali used to make me practice when we was waitin' for the school bus; he's my older brother."

"I know he's your brother, remember we went over your family history when we first met."

"Oh yeah, I forgot about that."

Weiss's smart phone chirped, he immediately removed it from his belt holster. "Yeah?" He paused. "Right, send him down, tell him we're making breakfast in the kitchen, use the side door then follow his nose."

Weiss laid the phone on the counter top. "Your partner's come to meet you."

"What partner?"

"The agent who'll accompany you on the mission, that partner."

"Okay; what's his name?"

"I'll let him introduce himself."

"He's an FBI agent like you?"

"Sort of; he's British. He'll tell you about that too." Doctor Weiss shoveled scrambled eggs, toast and sausages onto a plate and set the plate in front of Rusty. "Here, eat before it gets cold."

"Thanks." Rusty loaded the eggs with salt and pepper. "Aren't you havin' any?"

"I'll wait an' see if our guest's had breakfast. I can make more for myself."

Jasper quietly appeared in the kitchen doorway. "Good morning," he said.

Doctor Weiss turned away from the stove and extended his

hand. "Roger Biggs, FBI."

"Agent Biggs, a pleasure," Jasper responded. He nodded towards Rusty and the table. "And you are obviously Rustam Kas Samadi."

Rusty put down his fork, stood and held out his hand. "Rusty," he said, "it's Rusty."

Jasper shook hands and smiled. "Rusty, I'm Martin Jasper, I'm going to be your new best friend."

Rusty sat, looked Jasper over then grinned. "Yeah, an' maybe my last best friend."

TWENTY-TWO

Every officer on the ten-man Spanish Point police force had, at one time or another, come in contact with Jersey Buttcan, a homeless, registered sex offender who lived under a bridge ramp with a small group of sad, forgotten men and women. Buttcan's legal name, the name on his police rap sheet, was Jerzy Butshenko, but the police took pleasure in calling him Buttcan. Most of Buttcan's charged offences had been minor and all were non-violent: drunk and disorderly conduct, loitering, possession of a small amount of marijuana and drug paraphernalia. Even the sex conviction was a sort of misunderstanding. Three early-teen girls were wandering along the bank of the Caloosahatchee River near dusk, slugging on a fifth of cheap, cherry-flavored vodka. When they found Buttcan stoned, sitting on the edge of a decaying fishing pier, his worn, soiled clothing, ragged beard and long greasy hair offended their delicate adolescent sensibilities and they began to verbally taunt him. The most intoxicated of the three pulled down her halter top, exposing her budding breasts, and asked him if he remembered what tits looked like. (That, of course was conveniently omitted from the police report.) In his drugged haze, Buttcan stood, turned his back to the teens, lowered his trousers and under-shorts and *mooned* them; exposing his buttocks, but not his genitals. The girls screamed and ran away. Buttcan slowly pulled up his trousers and resumed his stoned reverie on the riverside pier.

The teen with the budding breasts was the daughter of a city councilwoman; if it had been otherwise, Buttcan most likely wouldn't have been convicted.

With a year in jail and the registered sex offender designation added to his rap sheet, Buttcan became a pariah. He was excluded from using the outdoor showers at the Living Redeemer Mission and barred from reading the newspapers and magazines on the outside porch of the public library. He was also prohibited from living within two hundred yards of a school or a residence with children under eighteen. The open space under the bridge approach was about the only place in the city available to Buttcan and his like and supermarket *dumpster diving* the primary source of his sustenance. Buttcan and the others who lived under the bridge did their best to tune out a hostile world by remaining continually drunk or stoned.

Buttcan thought the two clean-cut men, who appeared under the bridge one day, the men who gave him a pack of cigarettes and some *crack cocaine* rolled up in aluminum foil, were narcotics agents looking for information about drug dealers. He was dead wrong.

* * *

General Thornton was seated in the shade of a queen palm, relaxing on a park bench that faced the slow flowing river. Although the temperature was near ninety, the shade and a light breeze kept him from being uncomfortable. The sky to the northeast was beginning to turn gray. *Likely thunderstorm commin' in an hour or so,* he thought.

The path along the river's edge was flat and straight; several hundred feet to his left, he saw her emerge from the cover of a dense cluster of Areca Palms. She was dressed in a bright pink top and black running shorts, effortlessly jogging, taking large strides and bouncing on the balls of her feet, her long ponytail fluttering behind like a flag.

The General mentally pulled up an image of her naked, athletic body astride his pelvis, her full breasts rhythmically oscillating, reflecting the increasing urgency of her building orgasm; he smiled ear to ear.

She quickly covered the remaining distance to the bench and the seated General and halted before him. She placed her hands on her hips and exhaled. "Afternoon, Fidel," she said, not breathing hard. "Been here long?"

The General ignored her question and responded with his own. "Lookin' great, sergeant, you're still runnin' regularly?"

"Every day," she replied, "usually on the beach."

"Great to see you, it's been too long. Why don't you come out to Boca Grande and we can exercise together."

She grinned. "On the beach?"

"That too, if you insist; maybe go out for a nice dinner and I've got some of that special vodka you like."

"*Tito's Hand-Made*?"

"Yeah that's the one; I keep it just for you."

She tossed her head and unzipped her spandex top down to the sports bra that strained to control her full breasts. "When?"

"Next Saturday? I'm tied up with this project until then."

"Saturday; I think I can do that. I'll let you know when I report in tomorrow."

"I've got a meeting tomorrow afternoon; call as soon as you can."

She nodded. "You wana screw around some more or get down to business?"

He laughed. "You never change; always giving the orders. Your message said that you were set for tonight?"

"We picked up the package in Sarasota yesterday; the shoes and clothing. I personally checked out the big man our guy's replacing. Same height and build; our guy's maybe a little thinner, but that shouldn't be an issue."

"You got the wallet?"

"Yeah, that too; you want us to stick it in our guy's back pocket when we put him in the truck?"

The General shrugged. "Probably has a better chance of surviving the fire if you place it in the glove box."

"Okay, the glove box then."

The General frowned. "You sure this guy won't be missed; no

relatives to file a missing person report?"

"Like I told you, no relatives and no friends; he's a homeless druggie, a sexual predator with a long police record. He'll just disappear; happens with the homeless all the time."

"Police won't take notice?"

She grinned. "They'll notice and be real happy he left town. He's been shaved and had a decent hair cut. Like I said, he's the right size, only significant physical difference with your big man is that our guy has blue eyes instead of brown, but then after the accident and fire, no one will ever know the difference."

Fidel nodded. "Good job, we can talk about it next Saturday."

"On the beach," she replied and bounded off down the path.

* * *

The group was down to three. Avi Tesla had delivered the device to General Thornton's courier, and with his final payment deposited in a Swiss bank, he'd vanished into the anonymous sea of humanity. Avi was now a very wealthy man and would likely stay submerged for a long while, perhaps forever. Only Donner knew that Avi had once again changed his name, nationality, and passport.

For this last meeting there were no black file folders, and no Matilda Crane; the punch list was completed and all that remained was to execute the meticulously developed plan.

General Thornton was dressed in bright blue swim trunks and a plain, yellow tee shirt. He relaxed in a large rattan fan-backed chair on the screened porch of his winter home with a rum and Coke in his right hand, a Cuban cigar in his left, and his feet elevated on a colorful wicker hassock. Martin Jasper was more conventionally clothed in khaki trousers and a short-sleeved, blue oxford-cloth shirt, open at the neck. Jasper's sole concession to the subtropical climate was a pair of open-toed sandals. The

General's impressive home was built on concrete pilings and elevated fifteen feet above ground level. From the rear porch, the postcard-like view flowed across stalky, grass-covered sand dunes to the beach and the Gulf of Mexico.

The intercom blared a raspy message. "Doctor Donner and male companion in the drive," the guard at the entryway check-point announced.

"Got it," Thornton responded.

Jasper looked at his watch. "Ten minutes late, right on schedule; Nicholas insists on being the last to arrive. Perhaps we could go in now, away from this beastly humidity?"

"Let me just finish this exceptional cigar. I don't allow smoking in the house, but since I'm the only smoker and it's my house I suppose I could ignore my own rule."

"Rather you wouldn't, old fellow; thing smells like a cross between camel dung and old rope, I'd rather endure the humidity out here than the stink inside."

The General frowned and shook his head. "Limey aristocrats always gotta have things your own way; think you still rule the world."

"I'm a commoner, not a peer; you play at being the aristocrat more than I: this palace-of-sin, plus your Georgetown town house, and the stable of fast cars, not to mention your harem of expensive women."

Fidel laughed loudly. "Harem, huh? At my age I can't keep up with the harem anymore. All my female friends are fifty or older, at least the ones here on the island; Boca Grande isn't exactly South Beach, don't see too many thongs on this end of the beach."

The security system buzzed announcing a vehicle nearing the house. "So much for the cigar," the General mused, setting the half-smoked stump in a copper ashtray. "Let's get this over with," he declared as he pushed himself up from the chair and gestured toward the large sliders. "Air-conditioned inside, my lord, no beastly humidity and no cigars to offend your delicate sensibilities."

Jimmy and Donner were just exiting the elevator in the front hall. Both men wore dark trousers and white shirts but had removed their neckties and left them in the car along with their jackets. Jimmy was the more sartorially daring of the two; he'd left the top two shirt buttons open. Jimmy nodded to Thornton and Jasper then retreated toward the porch.

"Nasty out there," Jasper cautioned.

"Don't mind the heat," Jimmy replied, "I used to be a submariner."

"I don't know why in hell people want to live in this heat and humidity, gives me a headache," Donner said with a grin. "And put some clothes on, Fidel, I'm not used to meeting with old men in their underwear."

Thornton smiled. "I'm usually here only during the winter, when the heat helps keep the arthritis under control; you should try it."

"Never did like Florida," Donner grouched as he shook hands with Fidel. "Martin; glad to see you're wearing more than underwear." He extended his hand to Jasper.

"Nicholas," Jasper replied by way of greeting. "You just get in?"

"Flew into Punta Gorda, their little airport was a surprise; last time I flew in there was after the war, and the military airstrip was nearly abandoned. Now they can handle commercial jets. Against Kurt's advice and much to his chagrin, Jimmy picked up a rental car. With most of the people walking around nearly naked, didn't think there was much risk of getting shot at; I mean, where would they conceal a gun?"

"Drinks anyone?" the General asked. "I gave the staff a day off, but I think I can manage to open a beer or pour a glass of wine; I find rum and Coke best suits the climate."

"Not now," Jasper responded. "A glass of white wine would be lovely, but afterward."

"Not for me," Donner echoed. "Been having headaches all week long."

Fidel moved behind the long curly maple built-in bar at the far end of the room and refilled his rum and Coke. "Pansies," he teased as he saluted the other two with his fresh drink. He pointed to the doorway next to the bar. "We're in my office; video equipment's there."

Thirty minutes later, Thornton turned off the monitor and ejected the DVD. "Great stuff," he said enthusiastically. "Has he always had the scruffy beard?"

"It's only a month old," Jasper replied. "It'll look more natural in another few weeks."

Donner nodded. "The physical match with our requirements is good. How heavy was the mock-up under his robe—"

"*Ihram*," Jasper interrupted. "An ihram's the loose, two-piece garment men wear during the Hajj, not a robe."

Donner smirked then restated his question. "Was the mock-up underneath his *ihram* the same as the armed device he'll carry?"

"Exactly the same size, but seven pounds heavier," Jasper answered. "I thought that it looked quite natural, a well-cultivated beer belly, and he's had no difficulty carrying the weight."

"And he looks Aryan rather than Arab?"

Jasper nodded. "He does."

"That was Farsi he was speaking?"

"It was; Samadi's more intelligent than the video portrays; he's learned fast. The language coach says that his accent is acceptable, and since he had the remnants of a childhood vocabulary to build on, he's quickly mastered the basics he'll need to convince the few people he has to interact with that he's Iranian. Of course, he's far from fluent in the language; his capabilities are more like what you'd get from memorizing a phrase book."

"He understands the mission; he knows that he's going to blow himself up?" the General asked.

Jasper nodded. "Doctor Weiss, the DSC psychologist, has spent three weeks with Samadi, and he's totally convinced that Samadi is mentally prepared for a suicide mission. Samadi wants revenge, personal revenge for the murder of his wife. Curiously, Doctor Weiss feels that the mutilation of the cat is the event that pushed Samadi over the edge; Weiss believes that Samadi had come to accept his wife's murder as a tragic accident. Killing the cat was different, it was a brutal action directed specifically at Samadi, taunting him with the writing on the wall in the cat's blood; that's when Samadi went bonkers."

"Samadi is convinced Islamic terrorists killed his cat? He has no suspicion it could have been someone else?" Fidel asked.

"The FBI ruse was most successful," Jasper assured them. "Samadi believes that 'Agents' Johnston and Weiss are his allies and are acting on behalf of the United States Government. He's convinced the terrorists killed his cat. Samadi also believes the terrorists were indirectly responsible for the suicide of his coworker, the retarded man he calls Charley. Weiss's conjecture is that all of the emotions that Samadi had repressed over the murder of his wife, the wounding of his son and himself, and the suicide of his friend, explosively came together when Samadi found the mutilated body of the cat. That was the fuse that ignited a blind, consuming drive for revenge. Revenge against the terrorists is the only thing that matters to him now. He's written letters to be sent after his death, letters to his relatives and friends, letters full of hatred. . . Of course, those letters will be destroyed after we leave."

Donner painstakingly raised his arthritic body from the leather sofa and stood, hunched over the seated Martin Jasper. "I've read Weiss's report; but how about you, Martin, you've been with Samadi for several weeks. How do you feel? Is he ready to kill, to push the button?"

Jasper replied without hesitation. "I have no doubt that the poison that courses through his mind will make him push the button; he's ready, I'm sure."

Doctor Donner continued with Jasper. "What time are you leaving?"

"In the morning, at seven. We have several re-fueling stops before Sudan; then we go by boat from Port Sudan to Jeddah."

Donner nodded, clasped his hands behind his back, and walked toward the room's only window, a picture window with a view of the swimming pool and the lush, tropical palms and gardens. He paused for a few seconds then slowly turned on his heel toward the General. "The accident?"

"Last night, at about midnight, Samadi's pickup went off the road and ran into the piling of an interstate bridge in Charlotte County; about twenty miles from Samadi's home. Truck rolled over, caught fire, and burned the driver beyond recognition."

"Police have identified the remains?"

"Haven't heard yet, I'm expecting a call any time now. No need for concern though, my people don't make mistakes. The police will conclude its Samadi; white male in his mid-fifties, the same weight and height as Samadi."

"Where'd they get the body?" Donner asked.

Fidel faintly grimaced. "You don't need to know; no one who'll be missed."

"He was already dead?"

"Sure," the General said.

Donner started to pace between the leather couch and the window. "Why was Samadi twenty miles from home at midnight?"

Fidel shrugged and Jasper took over the narrative. "Probably on his way home from Key West. Before Johnston brought Samadi to the house in Sarasota, the house you saw in the DVD, Samadi told his friends in Lisson Grove that he'd be staying with his brother in Key West for a fortnight; he rang his son with the same story. While he was in Sarasota, he rang them both again to reinforce the story of his whereabouts."

Donner frowned. "How about his brother, won't he think it odd that Samadi wasn't in Key West?"

"We had Samadi call his brother; he talked to his sister-in-law actually, told her he needed to get away and was spending some time fishing with an unspecified friend in Fort Myers—"

"Not good," Donner interrupted. "Two different versions of Samadi's location, a weak link in the story."

"Not a big deal," the General began. "The police investigation will never get beyond the burned body in Samadi's pickup. We even planted some genuine ID that may have survived the fire; nothing to be concerned about."

"Damn it, Fidel, you know the success of our whole mission depends on Samadi cleanly vanishing from the earth."

General Thornton was getting visibly irritated and replied more forcefully. "Like I said, Nick, it's no big deal; I'll make sure the police investigation doesn't go beyond declaring that Samadi died in the accident; this is my territory, I call the shots."

Jasper stood. "I think we're quite finished here, gentlemen. Don't you agree? Now, Fidel, about that glass of chilled white wine you offered?"

TWENTY-THREE

"I promised Father, Ricky; promised I'd wait for him to tell Taylor and Sally, that's why I haven't said anything before now. But you've got to know all the details, and we both have to talk with Taylor right away."

"Nick's not expected to survive?"

"Matty said it was a massive brain aneurism, the doctors are amazed he's still alive."

"He's conscious?"

"Floating in and out, but not responsive, Matty said. He's on a respirator and hooked up with some other machines as well. Jimmy's at the hospital and Taylor and Gilly are on the way."

Cynthia had her hand on the lever of the front door.

"Just let me get my car keys," Rick said.

"No need, Matty's in Father's limo with Tilman; they should be out front by now."

"Walter Reed?"

"Umm," she replied. "Father was headed back from the Cabin when it happened. Tilman pulled over then called Jimmy; Jimmy was away so Tilman got to talk with Matty. She called a White House aide or somebody, who cleared Father through to Walter Reed—there they are!" she shouted, and the two of them ran down the steps to the double-parked black limo. As they climbed into the backseats, the single motorcycle escort pulled away with lights flashing and siren wailing.

Matilda Crane was in the front passenger seat, her long legs curled beneath her and a cell phone pressed against her ear. "You're sure?" she asked. She nodded several times. "Yes, she's here in the car; right, hold on." She held out the phone toward Cyn. "I'm so sorry, Cynthia; it's Jimmy."

Cyn set the phone to "speaker" mode. "Father's gone?" she asked.

Jimmy's normally animated voice was flat. "Five minutes ago; he died without regaining consciousness. I'm sorry to have to be the one to tell you, Miss Cynthia."

"I'm sorry for you, Jimmy; I know how much you cared for him; Taylor there?"

"He hasn't arrived yet."

"You have a pen and paper?"

"Yes, in my jacket pocket," he replied, as he fished out the small notebook.

"Listen carefully and please don't ask any questions. Ricky and I need to get to Boston as fast as possible; Matty, too. Where's the closest company plane?"

"Reagan National; there's a plane always ready for domestic flights. Tilman knows how to get to the terminal."

"Good, call and tell them we're on our way to the airport."

"Now?" Jimmy asked quizzically.

"Now, right away," she replied. "Then call Baynard Fulton, he's the chairman of the Bank of New England. Tell Baynard that Father's died and that I have to access his safe deposit box at the main office immediately. Tell him that I have the key and the documents to authorize opening the box, and we'll need transport from the airport to the bank when we get to Boston. Tell Baynard that if we're late I expect someone to be there to allow us to get into the box, no matter what time it is. . . Got that?"

"Yes, Ma'am," Jimmy replied with more animation.

"Then find Milton Tobias, Father's lawyer. He's likely to be on the golf course or playing poker in the locker room at his club, but you find him and tell him that it's urgent he call me; life-or-death urgent, got it?" Without waiting for a reply, Cyn continued. "Finally, the minute Taylor gets to the hospital tell him to call me; the minute he gets there. Now go!"

Cyn handed the phone back to Matty. "Can you contact that policeman and tell him we're going to the airport and won't need him anymore?"

"I'll take care of that," Tilman replied.

"Okay," Cyn announced as she pushed back into the seat, "now I guess you'll all wanna know what in hell's goin' on?"

TWENTY-FOUR

In Farsi, Saeed's name translated to "lucky or prosperous." It was an irony he often bitterly reflected upon while he maneuvered his taxicab through the traffic-choked streets and polluted air of Tehran; Saeed's life was anything but prosperous. Roqaya, his once-pretty, young wife had grown fat and lazy and was a terrible cook. When their apartment became overrun with dirty dishes, pots, and pans, and the laundry hamper overflowed with soiled clothing, Saeed would beat Roqaya. Then, for a time, she would sullenly clean, wash, and keep their home moderately neat until, once again, she'd let things go, and then Saeed would ultimately lose his temper and beat her. This pattern was as well established as the summer rains that fell on Saeed's boyhood home in the plains and valleys of the Zagros Mountains. Saeed's oldest child was an epileptic and had been diagnosed as retarded. At thirteen, he couldn't read nor could he remember more than a few simple prayers. Last year, Saeed had made the difficult decision to place his only son in a state institution for the feeble minded. Saeed's reclusive young daughter spent most of her waking hours sitting with her mother, staring at the TV, and barely acknowledged his presence when he returned home after a long day in the traffic, noise, and pollution.

Perhaps things were about to change for the better; perhaps Uncle Mohsen's gout attack was the will of Allah, and a gift to Saeed? Uncle Mohsen was rich and well connected with the Iranian leadership; he owned a factory in the south of the country. Uncle Mohsen was also kind, and when young Saeed's parents and sister were killed in a road accident, Uncle Mohsen had paid to send Saeed to boarding school rather than let him endure the hardships of a state-run orphanage.

Uncle Mohsen's phone call was totally unexpected, as was his offer to send Saeed to Makah, for the Hajj, in his place. Saeed was ecstatic! It was his opportunity, if only for a week or so, to leave the tedium and squalor of his small life and experience the grandeur of Makah and the Grand Mosque. More important, he would return from Makah a Hajji, one who had undertaken and completed the sacred pilgrimage that is every Muslim's duty. No one in Saeed's small circle of friends was Hajji. Of even more significance, not one of his wife's family members had yet undertaken the Hajj; at last, he would be entitled to some respect at their family gatherings when he would enthusiastically tell the stories of his adventures.

* * *

Saeed had had a whole month to anticipate the journey and to savor his good fortune, and now he was in his cab and on the way to meet his cousin Heydar at Mehrabad Airport. Heydar would be his companion to Makah and the Hajj. He hadn't seen Heydar since Uncle Mohsen's sixtieth birthday celebration three years ago in Shiraz. Heydar was forty; seven years younger than Saeed. Uncle Mohsen had adopted Heydar when he was a baby; a blue-eyed, blond-haired baby, a rarity among Iranian ethnic groups. As he'd aged, Heydar's hair turned a medium-brown color, but his eyes remained startlingly blue. Heydar was unmarried; Saeed, although he had only one specific experience to draw on, thought that Heydar was likely bisexual. Since in Iran homosexuality was punished by death, no one in the family ever openly speculated about Heydar's sexual orientation.

Although the official beginning of the Hajj was still several days away, the special Iran Air pilgrimage charter flights to King Abdul Aziz Airport in Jeddah were already in operation. During the next few weeks, more than sixty thousand of the faithful would fly from the major cities of Iran to complete their divine duty in Makah; many pilgrims would also travel before or after to Medina to pray at the Prophet's tomb in that holy city.

"Heydar, Heydar, over here!" Saeed called, pushing his large body through the crowd that surrounded the arrivals gate.

Heydar saw him and waved. When they met, Heydar embraced his cousin and kissed him warmly on both cheeks, and then on his lips. Saeed thought nothing of the greeting; Middle Eastern men were usually more physically intimate with each other than would be the case with Westerners.

"It's so good to see you, Saeed. You look just as I remember you, perhaps a bit fatter, but just the same."

Saeed laughed. "It's not Roqaya's cooking that's fattening me up, I can assure you. Her cooking is as bad as ever, maybe worse. And my dear uncle, he is suffering badly?"

"Not really, I think the gout was a convenient excuse to cancel the trip. He's made the Hajj twice before, you know. I think he decided to go one last time and booked the trip in a moment of religious fervor that quickly wore off when he remembered the physical toll the last Hajj took on his health. The hoard of pilgrims making the sacred journey over such a short time causes great physical stress on everyone, and an even greater strain on the elderly; better to go as fit young men like us."

"Fit like you, you mean. All I do is sit on my ass in the cab and get fat and flabby."

"You will be fine, Saeed. My father has us booked into the finest hotel in Makah, we have private transportation between the holy sites, and in the desert at Muzdalifah we will sleep in a private, air-conditioned tent; and, most important, in the Hajj terminal at the airport, we will be treated as dignitaries and will not have to endure the long queues at customs and passport control. Father does his holy duties in comfort. All of your travel documents are in order; Father used his contacts to have them quickly transferred from his name to yours. I have your passport as well. You brought the passport photos you will need for your ID cards?"

"As you told me, I have ten photos. You've been on the sacred pilgrimage before?"

Heydar shook his head. "Never, I was scheduled to accompany Father on his last, but there was a fire at the factory and I had to remain at home. Father went alone; I think that is why he found the journey so exhausting. I'm looking forward to the experience, those I know who have gone say that the Hajj is life transforming."

"I'm not particularly religious, but I too am looking forward to the experience," Saeed replied.

"We have more than three hours before we depart for Jeddah—let's find a place to get some coffee, a place where we can talk; there are things we need to discuss. Father is retiring this year and soon I will take over the management of the factory. I will need help, people I can trust, family. I thought that perhaps you might be willing to return to Shiraz and assist me?"

Saeed grinned. *"Beautiful Shiraz! Home! Away from Roqaya's family! Away from the noise and pollution of Tehran!"* Perhaps Allah was indeed smiling on him, perhaps he would become more religiously observant than he expected.

* * *

In Jeddah, the Airport Hajj terminal stretched out before them like a vast, marble lake covered above with the domes of white fiberglass tents, seemingly pitched in midair. It was one of the largest terminals in the world. For most of the year, the enormous Hajj terminal stood empty, but in a few more days, and for weeks to come, the terminal would pulsate with the movements and voices of hundreds of thousands of faithful Muslims, disgorged from aircraft constantly arriving from every part of the world. Today, days in advance of the official start of the Hajj, the massive terminal was relatively quiet, and the thousands of passengers currently entering the terminal were easily swallowed by cavernous entry halls and acres of purpose-designed space. Many pilgrims would undertake the shorter, optional Umrah prior to beginning the full Hajj.

Heydar and Saeed followed the multilingual signs the short distance to the Iran Hajj Ministry service desk where, after presenting their documents, they were shown into a comfortably furnished lounge reserved for special visitors. After a half-hour's wait, a young man in a perfectly tailored, white, Arab *thawb* approached Heydar.

"Mister Ganji, you speak English, do you not?"

Heydar nodded. "Yes, I speak English, but my cousin knows only Farsi."

"I am Hamza; I will be your *mutawwif,* your guide and helper while you are Allah's guest in our Kingdom. In the name of the Custodian of the Holy Shrines, I welcome you." Hamza returned their documents and handed each man a rubber bracelet and a security pin. "Please wear these at all times, my cell number is on the bracelet, you can call me at any time for assistance; please do not hesitate. According to the law, your passports will be retained here; I will personally assure that they are returned to you when you come back to this airport. This Hajj ID card will serve as your passport while you are with us. You may begin *ihram* here at the airport if you wish, places for you to wash, pray, and change are available."

Heydar shook his head. "We will begin at *miquat*, before we enter the holy city."

Hamza handed Heydar the picture IDs and their other travel documents and then led them through a side door, down a long hallway, and outdoors to a waiting Mercedes limo. Each man had only a single carry-on bag; after *niyyah talbiyah* prayers, they would begin ihram and change into the white, unstitched ihram garments and sandals they would wear throughout the entire Hajj.

Hamza stood in the doorway. "I will call you at your hotel this evening." He nodded and closed the door. The limo driver remained behind the wheel while a second man greeted them in Farsi, took their bags, ushered them into the rear of the limo, and then sat in the front passenger seat.

"How long will it take to travel to Makah?" Heydar asked, as the car pulled away from the terminal.

"If it is Allah's will, only one hour," the man in the passenger seat replied. "We will travel on the highway and then take a short detour around the site of a road accident that occurred an hour ago, a water truck collided with a bus; it will be much faster than waiting behind the backed-up taxi's and busses. We will have to stop for a police check of documents before we enter the holy city and will arrive at your hotel shortly afterward."

The broad highway stretched into the desert. They passed a number of busses packed with pilgrims, but traffic wasn't unusually heavy. The man in the passenger seat turned his head and spoke. "Starting tomorrow, there will be many more busses traveling to Makah, the road will be crowded and the journey will take much longer. You have come at a good time."

For half an hour they passed through uninteresting, flat desert terrain before the limo turned off onto an unpaved track. "We will travel this detour for only ten minutes before we rejoin the highway, just before the police checkpoint," the man in the passenger seat said.

The limo bumped over the obviously seldom-used sandy track for five minutes and then came to a halt. The man pointed to his watch. "It is time for afternoon prayer. This close to the holy city we must be especially observant. You will join with us? We have prayer rugs in the boot."

Heydar and Saeed stared at each other; Saeed shrugged. The driver and his companion stepped out and opened the rear doors. As Saeed and Heydar exited from opposite sides of the car, they saw that the driver and his helper each held a handgun at his side. The driver raised his arm and quickly fired three shots; his helper fired four, all head shots at point-blank range.

Saeed's and Heydar's lifeless bodies fell to the sand.

"Get their papers before they get bloodstained," the driver shouted across the roof of the limo. "And don't forget the bracelets and the pins."

After the bodies were stripped and thrown unceremoniously into a shallow grave, the driver wiped the sweat from his face and neck with a handkerchief. He took a large hedge trimmer from the trunk, bent into the grave, cleanly snipped two fingers from Heydar's right hand, then turned and cut two more fingers and a thumb from Saeed's corpse. He placed the fingers and thumb into two separate food storage bags, and casually tossed the gruesome treasure into the trunk. Both men spit into the grave; "Shia pigs," was all they said. The two men filled in the grave and returned the shovels and the cousin's bloodstained clothing to the limo's trunk, then turned the big Mercedes around and headed back to the highway.

* * *

The silver-and-white bus was pulled to the side of the road, the signs on the front and sides of the bus were lettered *SUDAN* in both Arabic and Roman script. The bus driver along with two men in grimy white robes stood on the pavement at the windowless rear of the bus. The Mercedes limo pulled to the side of the road and drove slowly up behind the bus to avoid attracting the attention of anyone aboard. From inside the car, the limo driver flipped open the trunk; the bus driver hurriedly took the shovels, bloodstained clothing, and gruesome plastic bags from the car's trunk and tossed everything into the luggage hold at the base of the bus. The driver handed Jasper a plastic bag containing clean garments. Jasper opened the bag, stripped and then he and Rusty quickly exchanged their soiled garments for similar, clean robes. They climbed into the back seat of the car while the bus driver quickly re-boarded the bus and drove away.

"Your photos." The man in the front passenger seat of the limo held out his hand.

Martin Jasper removed the green-and-black cap from his head and extracted two passport photos from the lining, which he placed in the man's extended hand. "Any problems?" Jasper asked in Arabic.

The driver chuckled. "Never knew what hit 'em."

The driver's helper took a small portable laminator from the glove box, plugged it into the cigarette lighter, and in less than five minutes had successfully attached Jasper's and Rusty's photos to the cousins' ID cards. He swiveled around in his seat.

"Saeed Habibi," he said as he held out an ID to Rusty. "And, with your blue eyes, you'd be Heydar," he said to Jasper. "Better put on these bracelets and security pins as well. Here are your other documents." He passed the papers to Rusty who handed them to Jasper. Jasper gave Rusty one of the rubber bracelets. "This is yours, Saeed."

"How much longer to the police checkpoint?" Jasper asked.

"Less than fifteen minutes," the driver replied.

"That's it then, no more English. We speak Farsi at the police checkpoint and at the miquat and hotel check-in as well—we're all Iranians now."

TWENTY-FIVE

"See that black, cube-shaped structure in the open courtyard of the mosque? That's the Ka'aba, the House of God." Martin Jasper pointed through the hotel's tenth-floor picture window. "It's the most sacred place in all of Islam, the place Muslims face when they pray from anywhere in the world. They say it was built in ancient times by the prophet Abraham and his son Ishmael; over the years, Muslims built the Masjid Al Haram, the Grand Mosque, around the Ka'aba. That's it, that's your target."

"Can I take off this thing now? The belt itches under my arm." Rusty was in the process of removing the upper half of the ihram garment that covered the lightweight mock-up of the bomb.

Jasper turned from the window. "Here, let me help you." He unlatched the buckles that fastened the flesh-colored nylon straps together at Rusty's chest and waist, and pulled the device away from Rusty's large torso. "There, that better?" Jasper asked as he laid the mock-up on the dining table.

"Them belts itch," Rusty complained. "I think it's the heat."

"You should be thankful that the Hajj doesn't occur in midsummer when temps are well over a hundred Fahrenheit every day." Jasper looked at the red mark under Rusty's right arm. "There's some ointment and talc in the bathroom that should take away the itch." Jasper lifted the bomb mock-up from the table. "Come with me, I'll put this thing in the bedroom closet and then put the salve on for you."

Rusty raised his arm and examined the red abrasion. "I can do it myself. Just put out the stuff."

"As you wish," Jasper coolly replied. "Just remember, if anyone comes to the door, anyone, for any reason, you go into the bathroom and lock the door behind you. We don't want anyone to see you without your big belly."

Rusty nodded. "Yeah, I know, I got it."

While Jasper carried the fake bomb to the bedroom, Rusty stared out of the window at the huge structure across the road from the hotel. The Grand Mosque reminded him of Giant's Stadium. When he was stationed at Fort Monmouth in New Jersey he'd traveled there with some army buddies to see an NFL game. But, in place of the stadium's white lines and green grass, the mosque's massive courtyard was paved with tiles that reflected dull-white, ice like, in the brilliant sunshine. The courtyard was completely enclosed within the walls of the mosque and surrounded by two raised tiers that looked to Rusty like stadium seating. Tall, slender towers rose into the sky from atop the walls.

"Quite a sight, isn't it?" Jasper had come back from the bedroom.

"I was just thinkin' it's like a gigantic football stadium. . . How many can it seat?"

"Never thought of the mosque as a stadium, but you're spot-on; it's New Wembley Stadium on steroids. Those aren't seats around the sides of the courtyard; they're open walkways pilgrims use to circle the Ka'aba when it gets too crowded to walk down below on the floor. There are a dozen or more halls for prayer under the walkways. Places for the pilgrims to pray before they enter the courtyard. They say that the Grand Mosque will hold over seven-hundred-thousand pilgrims, that's probably six or seven times Wembley or any American stadium."

"Why's it so big?"

"Wait 'til tomorrow, you'll see. They're cleaning the marble paving now, not so many Umrah pilgrims in the courtyard. Umrah is the minor pilgrimage, once the Hajj begins, a few million plan on circling round the Ka'aba."

Rusty grinned. "Won't they be surprised! Tell me again why they do this Hajj thing."

Jasper crossed in front of Rusty and peered intently at the mosque. "It's one of the things all Muslims have to do during their lives. The Sunni call it the Five Pillars of Islam: daily prayers, fasting, charity, and believing the truth of the writings in the Koran; those four things plus undertaking the Hajj."

Rusty grinned. "That's a lot of stuff for somebody to do. My wife was a Christian; she didn't have to do nothin' 'cept go to church. Lot a work bein' a Muslim. I can see why it's not so popular, why my father didn't bother with bein' a Muslim after he came to America."

"To the contrary my friend, it's the second largest and the fastest-growing religion in the world. Strictly speaking, Islam isn't just a faith or a religion; it's more a social and legal system that's bent on establishing a worldwide Islamic caliphate."

Rusty frowned. "What's a caliphate?"

"A universal, Islamic government run by the Imams and Ayatollahs and based on the archaic rules for human behavior set down in the Koran."

"Yeah, right. . .let's stick with this Hajj. So, the first thing they do is walk around that black thing seven times."

"*Tawaf,* circling the Ka'aba is called Tawaf."

Rusty grinned. "Not that I really need to know what else I'd have to do after I blow myself up, but let's see if I remember what you told me before: after the Muslims circle around the black thing seven times, they run back and forth between two hills, then go out in the desert an' climb up a mountain, say lots of prayers, sleep in air-conditioned tents in the desert, and then stone the Devil by throwing pebbles at some stone pillars—after that, they come back here to the mosque and walk around that black thing seven times again. I got that right? Wait, I forgot about the animal sacrifice and drinking the YumYum water."

Jasper laughed. "ZumZum, not YumYum. ZumZum's a sacred spring. Yours isn't exactly a scholarly description, old fellow, and you've mixed the Umrah, the minor pilgrimage, in with the Hajj, but you've got the general idea. The process is actually much more complicated; specific prayers are said during each phase of the Hajj and specific days and often specific times to visit each place. Stoning the Devil was particularly dangerous because it was considered most propitious for the pilgrims to throw their pebbles at the stone pillars, the pillars that represent Satan, on noon of the third day of the Hajj. So, thousands and thousands would surround the Devil pillars and throw stones from every direction, more often hitting other pilgrims than the Devil pillars. They changed the ritual a few years ago, now they fling their stones at three large walls, and from only one direction; much safer."

"If you ask me, this Hajj thing is pretty damned silly." Rusty was shaking his head. "Guess that's the kinda things they do to brainwash these Muslims an' turn 'em into terrorists."

"The Hajj is to reenact events Muslims think happened long ago to Abraham, his wife, and son, and to the prophet Mohamed; like when the Devil tried to tempt Abraham three times and Abraham threw stones at the Devil and chased him away. Understand, Islam is a relatively new world religion, didn't start until about six or seven centuries after Christianity. Some religious historians think that many of the rituals of the Hajj are based on the ceremonies of earlier desert people who lived in this area, people who worshiped local gods before Islam developed and before Mecca was settled. There's a sacred black stone, probably an asteroid, that's set into one of the corners of the Ka'aba; likely something from one of these ancient societies."

"That's what I gotta get near, right, that black stone?"

"That's your goal," Jasper replied. "It'll be a challenge, masses of pilgrims will be trying to get up to the stone, to kiss it or rub it, likely to be a lot of pushing and shoving. Actually, it doesn't matter if you get that close; as long as you're within fifty or sixty yards, the explosion will take out the entire Ka'aba, black stone and all."

"Wish I could see the instant replay!"

"I expect that everyone on earth will see the replay. You're sure you're ready; we go tomorrow morning?"

Rusty put his hands on Jasper's shoulders and gently shook him. "Martin, I been a dead man since they shot my wife. Jus' took what they did to Charley and to poor Tater for me to understand how evil they are, how I need to kill the bastards. I'm already dead inside; tomorrow what's left of me'll finish what they started." Rusty released Jasper and smiled broadly. "Now, when we gonna eat supper, I'm startin' to get hungry."

"After *magrib* prayers, at sunset," Jasper answered. "I've booked us at the Al Qasr restaurant here in the hotel; it has an excellent reputation. You'll have to put on your belly and speak Farsi."

"Last meal on death row, huh? I get to order anything I want, right?"

Ignoring the attempted gallows humor, Jasper replied, "We'll have breakfast up here tomorrow morning. The bomb won't arrive until ten."

As if to change the subject, Rusty looked around the room. "This place must cost a lot of money; the poor slobs that was with us on the boat from Sudan couldn't pay to stay in a place like this; those guys really stunk, had to hold my breath sometimes."

"Most of the Hajj pilgrims are extremely poor; they have to save for years to afford the journey. Often families pool their cash and send a representative, knowing that most family members will never make it to Mecca. Farther back from this hotel, away from the Grand Mosque, are many rather nasty 'hostels,' places with small rooms, bed rolls on floors, and squat toilets. During Hajj, they stuff six or eight pilgrims in each room, sometimes more. Hotels like this one are for the privileged. The Mecca Palace is favored by the Iranian elite and other important Shia; wealthy Americans and Asians often choose the Intercontinental."

"Tell me again, what's the other kinda Muslims called, not the Shia, the other ones?"

"Sunni," Jasper answered. "Most of the world's Muslims are Sunni, about ninety percent—"

"I get it," Rusty interrupted. "They're like the Catholics and the Baptists, these Sunni and Shia. There's lots of Catholics around the world, but not so many Baptists. Charley was a Catholic, but he never had a good word to say about the Baptists, even though they all was Christians."

Jasper shook his head. "It's a lot more serious with the Shia and the Sunni, deep down inside they despise each other. It goes back centuries to when the Prophet Mohamed founded Islam. After Mohamed died one group of his followers recognized the father of Mohamed's principal wife as the new head of the religion; they became the Sunni. Another group took the position that Mohamed's cousin Ali was Mohamed's rightful successor, and they became the Shia. Over the next century and a half there were frequent battles and wars between the Shia and the Sunni. Although they're both part of Islam, serious differences in beliefs and practices keep them set against each other. Almost all of the people living in Iran are Shia, and nearly everyone in Saudi Arabia is Sunni. Since the Saudis control access to the holy cities of Mecca and Medina, when it comes to the Hajj pilgrimage, there's always been considerable friction between Sunni Saudi Arabia and Shiite Iran. For hundreds of years, Muslim blood has been spilled on the way to the Hajj and at the Hajj as well. As recently as nineteen-eighty-seven, Iranian Shia protesters fought against Saudi security forces here in Mecca; more than four hundred died. And, in nineteen-seventy-nine, armed, extremist, Islamic forces captured the Grand Mosque during Hajj and held thousands of pilgrims captive for nearly ten days. There was some conjecture at the time that the bin Laden family, Osama's family, was involved; their construction company was in the process of remodeling portions of the Grand Mosque and could easily have smuggled weapons in."

"How come you know so much about Muslims?"

"At university I studied the peoples who live here in the Middle East; learned their languages, histories, and their cultures. I lived and worked in Syria and Lebanon and traveled to all of the countries in the region."

"Why'd you ever wanna do a thing like that?"

Jasper shrugged. "Really, don't know; seemed an exciting life at the time—more interesting than litigating divorce settlements or trading equities. Why did you become a garbage man?"

"Dunno, maybe 'cause nobody else wanted the job."

"Perhaps that's what happened to me," Jasper nearly whispered. "Nobody wanted the job."

TWENTY-SIX

A stunned General Thornton was still dressed in his tracksuit. He got the call at the gym, and quickly pulled on the tracksuit over his sweaty tee and shorts, then jogged to the Crystal City Metro station. Twenty minutes and three stops later, the train pulled into L'Enfant Plaza. Thornton avoided the stairs and escalators that led from the Metro exit to the street, and instead followed the signs to the L'Enfant Plaza Hotel; the hotel was built directly over the metro stop and was a favorite with visitors to the nearby Smithsonian museums.

The man was standing to the side of the lobby coffee kiosk; he was dressed in a well-tailored dark suit and had a mini-phone plug in his ear. Thornton had entered the hotel lobby from the stairs rather than the elevator and saw the man before the man noticed him. He stayed to the man's left, out of his line of sight as he approached.

"Good Morning, General," the man said with a grin as he continued to look straight ahead.

Thornton placed his right hand on the man's shoulder. "Haven't lost the touch I see."

The man turned crisply on his heel, and shook the General's outstretched hand. "Thanks for saying so, sir. It's a great pleasure to see you once again."

"Desert Storm, I think was the last time. He's here, Major?"

"Actually, it's Colonel now, sir, and yes, he's waiting in the car; you'll follow me, please."

The two men exited the hotel from the main entrance, the colonel leading the way toward a modified, black Cadillac Escalade with heavily tinted windows, parked at the curb with the engine running. "You'll pardon me for not saluting, sir," the colonel said as he opened the rear door.

"Great to see you again, son," Thornton replied and slid into the van while the colonel circled around the vehicle, took the front passenger seat, and raised the glass privacy panel between the front and rear seats. The driver pulled the Escalade away from the hotel and took a left turn toward the interstate.

"Mister Secretary." Thornton nodded toward the slim, silver-haired man who was pushed back in the corner, huddled against the chill under a tartan blanket.

"Good of you to come so quickly, Fidel. I was greatly saddened to hear of Nicholas' untimely death. I'll inform the President when I meet with him this afternoon; if he hasn't already heard."

"Thank you for calling, sir; Nicholas was a lifelong friend and a loyal American."

The Secretary nodded. "Yes, he was that all right—there'll be no impact on the operation?"

Fidel shook his head. "None whatsoever: Nick's part was finished when Goldilocks and Mama Bear got on the plane."

The Secretary frowned. "Who invented the stupid names?"

"Nick did; you'll remember he had a nerdy sense of humor."

"When will it happen?"

"Mecca's seven hours ahead of Eastern; it'll be between three and four, our time, tomorrow morning."

"You've spoken with Goldilocks?"

Fidel grinned. "Actually, Mama Bear is the minder, and yes, I've talked with him. They're at the hotel, the device has arrived in Mecca, and everything's on schedule. I won't communicate with him again unless there's a problem on his end; Saudi phone network's too porous. You're expecting a violent anti-American reaction?"

"We are; contingency plans are in place, though not specific to this operation of course. Let's hope it doesn't take the incompetent bastards too long to follow the clues to the mother lode."

The General broke out into a broad grin. "Nothing to worry about on that end; Mama Bear's dropped a trail of breadcrumbs leading right to Hezbollah's front door and—"

The Secretary interrupted. "You understand the time criticality? All these so-called Arab Spring revolutions have clearly destabilized the entire Middle East."

"Mister Secretary, the Saudis will have every incentive to move the investigation forward at lightning speed. The Islamic world will be screaming for revenge and the world media will report every detail twenty-four-seven. Initially, the Saudis are gonna look real bad. The pressure on them, as caretakers of the holy cities and the Grand Mosque, will be immense; I don't think they can screw this one up."

The Secretary sneezed loudly and somberly shook his head. "Let's pray you're right. I understand you fixed the problem with the pilgrim, the one our mule's replacing?"

"We lucked out. The Iranian pilgrim we selected runs a munitions factory and is part of the Iranian government's inner circle. He was to go on the Hajj with his son but he got sick and had his nephew take his place. Lucky for us, the nephew is a big man about the same size as the original pilgrim, *and,* more important, the same size as our mule. The original pilgrim's son traveled from Iran with the nephew, and after the two of them arrived in Jeddah they were both cleanly replaced by the mule and his minder. The Mecca hotel suite the Iranian cousins reserved, the suite where our two guys are staying, will be wiped clean, then we'll plant fingerprints from the son and the nephew around the suite—like the son and nephew stayed at the hotel and our mule and his minder never existed."

The Secretary opened his mouth to ask the obvious question about the fingerprints; Thornton cut him off, "You wouldn't want to know."

It had begun to drizzle; the two men gazed silently out of the windows for several minutes until the Secretary spoke, "Thought we'd name a building after Nick, something to do with technology, he'd like that. Anything I can do for you?"

"Well, Tommy, old pal, maybe you could get me a seat in an F-15 when the curtain goes up on the final act?"

The Secretary laughed and slowly shook his head. "Fidel, there's about as much chance of that happening, as me gettin' a second shot at the Rose Bowl. Now, old friend, where can I drop you?"

General Thornton's cell phone chirped. He took the phone from his zippered tracksuit pocket, flipped it open, and checked the caller ID: "Jimmy, Nick's aide; I think I should take this."

The Secretary nodded.

"Yeah, Jimmy."

"It's Cynthia; she wants to take a company plane to Boston."

Thornton put the phone in "speaker" mode. "Didn't get that, you said something about Cynthia and a plane to Boston?"

"That's what I said. Cynthia, her husband, and Mrs. Crane are in Doctor D's limo on the way to Reagan National. She just called; told me to phone the DSC aviation manager, then Tobias, Doctor D's lawyer; she wants to get into the doctor's safe deposit box when she gets to Boston."

"You called the lawyer?"

"Not yet, figured you'd want to know first."

"Good man; call the DSC aviation manager, tell him to stall; tell Cynthia something plausible about weather delay, mechanical problems, something that sounds good."

"Shall I call the lawyer in Boston?"

"Not yet; let me work on this and call you back in ten."

"Got it," Jimmy replied and hung up.

Thornton returned the phone to his pocket.

The Secretary took a wad of tissues from the box that sat next to him on the seat, *Ketchoo!* He sneezed loudly. "God-Damned flu," he cursed, then blew his nose. "You knew about Nick's safe deposit box in Boston?"

Thornton shook his head. "Nicholas never mentioned a safe deposit box."

"Obviously he told his daughter about a box."

"Yeah, and she obviously thinks it's pretty urgent for her to get hold of the contents; Nick's body not even cold yet. I'm positive Nick never told her anything about the operation; it's the crowning achievement of his life's work. I mean, he wasn't even that close with Cynthia; they hardly saw each other."

"It's distasteful to me, Fidel, but I think we need to put Nick's daughter and the other two in protective custody until tomorrow when this is over. The only other approach would be to interrogate them, and that seems a fool's errand; I'm as sure as you that Nick never disclosed any information to his daughter or to anyone else. Unlikely the safe deposit box has anything to do with this operation; nonetheless, I'll get Justice to come up with a reason to temporarily seal the box; shouldn't be difficult with Nick having just passed away; not unusual for deposit boxes to get sealed after a death."

* * *

Gillian Donner pulled her cream-colored Range Rover to a screeching halt on the damp pavement outside the DSC flight operations office at Reagan National. Taylor jumped from the passenger seat, left the door wide open, and sprinted the twenty-five yards into the building. He was surprised to find Rick alone in the small waiting room. "Where're the women?" he hollered.

"Ladies' room," a stunned Rick replied, and pointed toward the rear of the small lounge.

Taylor bounded to the unisex restroom and pulled open the door. Matty Crane was repairing her makeup in front of the mirror. "Where's Cyn?" he demanded.

Matty abruptly turned from the mirror and wordlessly pointed at a toilet stall. "Cyn, get out here—now!" Taylor ordered. "No time to explain, we've got to get out of here right away; you too, Matty!"

Taylor turned and strode back to the lounge where Rick was standing with his hands on hips. "What in hell's goin' on, Taylor?" he asked.

"Go out to the car; no time to explain. Feds are coming to put you in protective custody, you and the women."

Cynthia and Matty stumbled out of the restroom. Cyn opened her mouth, but before she could speak, Taylor pushed open the outer door and pointed to the SUV. "Outside, get in the car, both of you; I'll explain in the car."

The two women piled into the rear seat with Rick. Taylor jumped in the front, slammed the door, while Gillian accelerated hard. The tires squealed loudly and the rear spun sideways. "Always wanted to see if this old tank could do that," Gilly said with a grin, as she powered toward the exit.

"I don't understand," Rick said to Taylor. "You said protective custody; protective custody from whom?"

"Protective custody?" Cynthia nearly shouted.

As best he could, Taylor twisted his body around in the tall bucket seat to face the three passengers in rear seats. "No need to go to Boston for Father's safe deposit box, there's nothing in it; Gilly and I flew up and emptied the box two days ago."

"Uh-oh, we've got a tail," Gilly announced. "Dark green van followed us from the DSC aviation office, I noticed it when we cleared the area, and the van never stopped at the airport, just turned and followed us."

"Can you lose him?" Taylor asked.

"I'd guess a minivan versus this old tank is probably an even match, let's see who's the better driver."

"Relax," Taylor announced to those in the rear seat, "Gilly's father taught her to drive; he trained to be a Formula One driver."

Gilly was hitting ninety halfway up the I-395 on-ramp. "You three should buckle up; you too, Taylor, just in case we slide around a bit."

"Slide!" Cyn shouted. "Slide where?"

"He's still there; I'll try to squeeze him out at an exit." Gilly turned her head toward Taylor, 8B's next?"

"Two and a half miles."

"And then the one after?"

"8C for the Pentagon, that's another couple miles."

"8C has a two-lane exit, doesn't it?"

"Don't remember."

From the rear seats Rick looked at the speedometer; she was doing over a hundred. "Two lanes," he said, "8C's a two-lane exit."

"Great, let's try 8C. First, let's get this geezer to close up."

Gilly punched the accelerator; the big V-8 still had enough power left to surge forward. Gilly was weaving in and out of lanes, passing vehicles on both sides. She pulled on the wheel and nearly spun from the outside lane across two others to the second from the inside lane. Cyn audibly gasped.

"C'mon, c'mon, stay with me!" Gilly shouted. "Move your bloomin' arse!"

Gilly backed off the power and slowed the Range Rover to near the speed limit; the green van braked hard to avoid rear-ending the SUV. She pulled up alongside the front of the cab of a big semi traveling along in the outside lane at about 65. "Now," she shouted. "Hang on!" She stabbed the accelerator, pulled the wheel hard right, shot around the front of the semi, missing its huge chromed bumper seemingly by inches, and just made it into the last thirty feet of the fast disappearing exit lane. "Sucker!" she called, as the green van hurtled by the semi and the exit. "Everyone okay?"

"I think I might have peed myself," Cyn calmly replied.

* * *

Matty stood off to the side making coffee while the others sat around the oval, mahogany table in the conference room that adjoined Taylor's office. "I'm still not sure I got this right," Cyn frowned. "Father and Fidel have been working with the Federal Government for years."

Taylor shook his head. "No, that's incorrect. The United States Government had nothing to do with my father's clandestine activities; neither Father nor the General took direction from anyone in our government, and their activities were never funded, directly or indirectly, by any government agency. Other than Father's occasional use of company aircraft, DSC was never actively involved in their projects either; everything they've done was on their own initiative and with their own nickel."

"I'm confused," Cynthia sulked.

Taylor inhaled then deeply exhaled. "Sorry, Cyn, I've been jumping all over the place and not doing too good a job explaining. Let's try again from the beginning—Father and Fidel were very well connected, in this country and in many others. After Fidel retired from active duty, he approached Father with an idea, a plan to right some specific wrong and assist the interests of the United States in the process. I don't know the details of that first operation; Father's journals don't go back that far. If I had to guess, I'd say their early projects were in Central America and involved battling the drug lords."

"So this has been going on for a long time?"

"I figure about fifteen-sixteen years; counting from when Fidel retired. At least ten separate interventions—"

"But you never knew?" Cyn interrupted.

"I didn't. Father was a genius at compartmentalizing his life. Before I took over as CEO, he talked with me all the time about everything going on at DSC, but never about other aspects of his life. Given my childhood experience with an 'absentee father,' I never thought his behavior especially peculiar. The first time I knew Father was involved in something outside of DSC was when Matty told me about the file she'd seen with the reference to a dirty bomb. I figured that the dirty bomb in the file must have had something to do with an agency or department bid for a study or assessment. When Father got wind of an upcoming business opportunity for DSC, he'd usually call a division VP, a manager, or just as likely, a long-time employee who Father knew had expertise in the area of the opportunity. About half of his 'opportunities' never went anywhere; the other half ranged from bids on small jobs to collaborations on major projects. From the day he started the company, Father was always looking for new business. Since I've been CEO, often, but not always, Father would tell Jimmy to send me an e-mail explaining who in DSC Father had contacted; but over the last year, I'd been getting fewer of those e-mails. Matty's heads-up about an RDD, a dirty bomb, caught my attention; I know DSC's competencies and capabilities as well as anyone, including Father, and was sure that taking on any type of assessment or study on an RDD wasn't in our skill set. So, I called Jimmy and asked if Father had contacted anyone about an RDD. Jimmy said absolutely not, he was positive. I didn't know what to think and called Matty."

Matty turned from making coffee and took a seat. "And I told Taylor that Jimmy was lying. Jimmy always prepared the reports that went into the black folders, typed them himself, he knew there was a reference to an RDD in the Arlington meeting's report. . . Coffee will be ready in a few."

Taylor nodded. "I checked with all the division VPs and no one was doing anything about an RDD, not a study, not a response to an RFP, nothing."

"RFP?" Cyn asked.

"Request for Proposal," Rick replied. "How most government agencies get companies to bid on projects."

"Okay, okay; but, why were the goons in the green van gonna put us in protective custody?"

"Tilman called me in the car when Gilly and I were headed to the hospital. Tilman said that just after he'd dropped the three of you off at the airport, some government agents in a green van had turned on their flashing lights and pulled him over. They wanted to know where you were, said that you were in some danger and that they needed to protect you."

"We were nearby and decided to come get you before they did," Gilly added.

"But—"

Taylor cut Cynthia off. "I knew Jimmy had called to tell you Father was dead. When Tilman said you were going to Boston, I was sure that you were going after the safe deposit box and Father's journals. What you didn't know was that Father called me two days ago to tell me that he was nearly blind and didn't think he would live much longer."

"You knew he was dying, the brain cancer?" Cyn asked.

Taylor slowly shook his head. "Not from Father, he never said a word, not until then."

"I'm sorry, Tay; he made me promise not to tell anyone, not even you or Ricky. He thought that he had months more to live. I'm sorry, I should have said—"

"No problem," Taylor interrupted. "Father didn't tell me, but I've known about his brain tumor for a month. Doctor Volpeck is Father's primary-care physician; mine, too. When I went in for my semi-annual checkup, she rather innocently asked about Father's status. You see, since the initial diagnosis, Father's been in the care of specialists. I guess they send her reports; but she has a busy practice and didn't know his current status."

"Finish the story, Taylor." Gilly smiled, and then stood and patted Matty's shoulder. "I'll pour the coffee."

"Okay, where was I?"

"Boston, safe deposit box," Rick replied.

"Yeah; when Father called he said that it was urgent for me to get hold of his journals from the safe deposit box in Boston. I called my Grand Prix-driver wife and we took a company plane to Boston. We had lunch at CeCe's, filled up a medium-size suitcase with Father's journals and papers, and headed home."

"A most pleasant day," Gilly chipped in.

"Next morning I went to visit Father at the Cabin; he was completely blind. Jimmy had dressed him and fed him breakfast. Father was disoriented, but still making sense. We talked for an hour, only about his journals. He was unemotional and seemed intellectually detached from his blindness and imminent death. When I left, he kissed me on the cheek and asked my forgiveness for his gross negligence as a father. I think that we were both pleased that he couldn't see the tears running down my cheeks." Taylor lowered his head; Gillian returned to her seat, covered his hand with hers and picked up the narrative.

"So, Taylor called me on the car phone and told me to start reading Nick's journals, starting with the most recent. It wasn't an easy job, I'll tell you; Nick's handwriting's like chicken scratches in the sand. By the time Taylor got home, I'd made an outline of the juicy bits; read like a paperback novel, it did."

Taylor cleared his throat. "Fidel's operatives have an RDD, a *very* dirty bomb. They're going to detonate it this evening or tomorrow morning during the annual Hajj pilgrimage at the Grand Mosque in Mecca, the Muslim Holy-of-Holies. It'll make the Mosque inaccessible to humans for years, maybe a decade."

No one spoke; the wall clock ticked; the coffeemaker spat out a few sizzling drops onto the warming plate below.

Rick found his voice first. "Why? Why would they do that? Do Nick and Fidel hate Muslims that much; is this about revenge, revenge for Nine-Eleven?"

Taylor looked straight ahead, his eyes seemingly fixed at a spot on the far wall. "Nothing to do with hate, or revenge, or Islam, or for that matter, any religion; it's about power—power and influence. The balance of power in the Middle East is undergoing a colossal shift: the Arab Spring removed the strongmen, the brutal dictators, the only ones holding the Islamist extremists at bay; the potential of a nuclear-armed Iran; the loss of Saudi and American influence and prestige throughout the region. Father and General Thornton discovered a way to turn the whole damn mess around, and to the advantage of the United States of America."

Cynthia shivered. "Bombing a Mosque, killing thousands of innocents; that'll shift the balance of power?"

Taylor shifted his gaze and stared hard into Cyn's eyes. He shook his head. "It's a brilliant plan, Cyn; Father and Fidel are starting a war between Muslims; setting up Iran as the patsy, pinning responsibility for the Mosque attack on the Iranians, isolating Iran from the rest of the Islamic world. Brilliant; the Saudis and the Arab States get carte blanche to disembowel their ancient Shia enemy; the United States regains its strategic influence in the area; everyone wins, everyone except Iran and—"

Gilly interrupted. "Do the Sunni and the Shia really hate each other that much, enough to go to war and kill each other?"

"The Shia and Sunni despise each other with an intensity that's second only to the hatred they both have for the Jews. It won't be the first time they've shed each other's blood in anger."

Rick stood. "They're complicit, the Saudis?"

Taylor nodded.

"And the United States Government?"

"Uninvolved," Taylor answered.

"And unaware?"

"Unaware," Taylor softly replied. He lowered his head and breathed out through his nose before continuing. "There's more to it. My father and Fidel firmly believe that all of Islamic State's hideous atrocities, the beheadings, mass executions of Christians and human immolations have the express purpose of luring the United States into a larger Middle Eastern war, a war that would pit America, the West and Christians against Muslims. It would become a war that would gradually entice moderate Muslims to join with the Islamic Extremists against a common, materialistic, infidel, enemy. Father believed that starting with Vietnam the United States has been screwing up foreign military engagements, sacrificing the lives of our brave young men for little advantage to our country; he didn't want that to happen again and on what could be a horrific scale. Father and Fidel decided to overstep what they saw as the inaction and failure of the United States Government in the Middle East; they decided to take their own executive action. "

Cyn had trouble finding her voice and started hesitantly, "W-what are we gonna do? Tonight, you said, they're setting off the bomb tonight; there's not much time to stop them!"

"Too late," Taylor forcefully responded. "We can't do a thing to stop it; not a friggin' thing."

Cynthia violently shook her head. "We have to do something; you can't just let all those innocent people die!"

"It's too late," Taylor repeated. "No one can stop it now."

"You can call someone; you and Ricky know every important decision maker in this town."

Taylor half smiled. "And what would I say? My father, along with a decorated Major General and some looney associates have smuggled a dirty bomb into the Grand Mosque and are going to detonate it any minute now? You think anyone would take me seriously? They'd figure I was drunk, or worse, stoned out of my mind. It's too late, Cyn, there's no nine-one-one to call for this sort of thing."

Cynthia's face was ashen. "This is insane! Father and Fidel are terrorists, mass murderers, indiscriminant killers, murderers, terrorists; don't you understand?" She pushed back in her chair. "I'm gonna be sick," she cried, and ran for the private bathroom in Taylor's office.

Rick turned to follow her.

Taylor rose to his feet. "You do understand, Rick; we couldn't stop what my Father's put in place even if we wanted to? And, we don't want it stopped; do we?"

Rick stared at the oval table.

Taylor nearly shouted, "The damage to Donner Systems, to my reputation and yours as well would be catastrophic. You do understand? There's no way out!"

Rick locked eyes with Taylor. "Cyn got it right; your father's a terrorist, not a patriotic hero, just a soul-less terrorist, no different than the suicide bombers who kill innocent women and children. . . I need to see to my wife." He calmly turned on his heel and left the conference room.

Rick softly tapped on the bathroom door. "You okay?"

"I'll be alright," Cyn replied weakly.

"Sick to your stomach?"

"No, I just had to get out of that room, I was suffocating."

Rick heard the toilet flush. "Anything I can do for you?"

"Just give me a minute to get myself together."

Rick heard the water run in the wash basin.

When, after a few minutes Cynthia hadn't opened the door, Rick knocked again. "Sure you're all right?" She didn't answer so he tried the door; it wasn't locked. He opened the door a slit. "Cyn?"

"I'm still here," she replied.

He opened the door a bit further; she had closed the lid and was seated on the toilet. There were no red eyes or tear lines through her makeup. "You can come in," she said. "I'm okay now; I just need to compose myself. Taylor's right, of course; it is too late, there's no way we could stop Fidel and his men—it sickens and disgusts me, but I understand that nothing can be done. What's really gnawing at me is the clinical detachment of all of you; Father, Taylor, and you too, Ricky. Any minute now, hundreds of innocents will be blown to bits and you all seem to think this is something to celebrate. This was Father's rotten way of life, Ricky—not yours or mine."

Rick lowered himself to one knee and took her hands in his.

"We're going home, Mrs. Cappa, home to *The Point*. I've put my company up for sale; I'm not gonna peddle influence for anyone again. You're healthy now and getting stronger by the day; you're the only one who matters to me. I love you, Cyn, I've always loved you; we're going home, home to start a real life, just you and me; away from the beltway, the Nicks, Fidels, the politicians and DSCs."

A radiant smile spread across Cyn's face. "I accept," she purred. Her eyes explored the space in the small bathroom. "Do you always choose such romantic settings for your proposals?"

She lowered her forehead to touch his.

"Com'on, let's get the hell out a here," Rick said.

TWENTY-SEVEN

Mu was standing on a closely mown lawn, directly in front of an orange grove. The orange trees were of uniform size and shape and stretched in neat rows toward the horizon. Mu wore a long, flowing white gown that billowed around her feet and, driven by a gentle breeze, played along the tops of the grasses. Tater was larger than he had been in life, the size of a small sheep; that was it, a lamb. He sat sphinx-like in front of Mu, his front paws curled under his chest, his eyes fixed forward in a curious stare. The light was intense, it made Rusty squint. It wasn't obvious whether the light was radiating outward from the scene, or shining into it from an unseen source. Mu's dark hair hung forward, over her shoulders; her hair was much longer than Rusty had ever seen him, wear it in life. Her face was glowing, and her full smile, luminous. Without opening her mouth or speaking she softly called to him. "Come to me. Come to me now." As soon as Mu spoke, the landscape began to fade and darken, and Mu held out her hand. "Take my hand, don't ever let go!" Mu's fingers and arm elongated and seemed to extend beyond the boundaries of the scene.

Rusty reached out; he strained to find Mu's hand. The muscles in his upper arm burned and felt as if his arm were about to separate from his shoulder. He cried out, "I can't find you, help me!" And then their fingertips touched and her large hand slid softly into his. "Don't ever let go," she cried once again, her voice fading away in the darkness.

* * *

Rusty was still in the habit of rising early and woke before the first rays of the sun fell upon the Ka'aba. He felt the warmth of Mu's hand, the stimulation where she had stroked the back of his hand with her thumb; he knew it had been more than a dream, it was a command. He smiled and energetically pushed out of bed; he was anxious to be on his way.

Rusty brushed his teeth, showered, then pulled on a pair of boxer shorts. Martin Jasper was still lightly snoring in the second double bed when Rusty left the room and walked to the living-dining room. Rusty moved a chair from the table and set it in front of the big picture window so he could watch the Grand Mosque come to life. The square in front of the mosque was already crowded with those ready to perform the Morning Prayer and others were rushing to join them. As the crowd grew, the individual men at prayer vanished and a great, white wave took shape, a white wave that was punctuated, here and there, with women clothed in black instead of the men's white ihram garment. Rusty felt that he was looking down onto a vast community of colorless insects, insects following a genetically programmed ritual. He realized that Jasper hadn't exaggerated; today, the Grand Mosque would host hundreds of thousands of pilgrims. Today, an infidel would invade this most sacred place, walk among the faithful, and exact a terrible revenge on Muslims and their god. Rusty smiled.

For over an hour, Rusty sat motionless and watched, transfixed, as the sun slowly rose and the pilgrims began their inexorable flow through the mosque and into the immense courtyard, circling the Ka'aba counterclockwise, like a white river, lapping against the black House of God.

"Ah, here you are." Jasper was dressed in a light-blue silken dressing robe with an embroidered hotel crest on the left breast pocket. "Couldn't sleep?"

"Slept fine," Rusty replied, without turning his gaze from the window. "Jus' wanted to see the show from the beginnin'; you seen this before?"

Jasper shook his head. "Mecca's a closed city; against the law for anyone but Muslims to enter. Not just during the Hajj, anytime. That was what the police stop was all about; check our papers, make sure we were Muslims."

"Then you're not really a Muslim?"

"Whatever gave you the idea I was?"

"You know a lot about the religion, the Hajj, the mosque; stuff like that."

"As I said before, when I was younger, I lived in Damascus and toyed with the idea of converting. At that time I was in awe of all things Middle Eastern. I considered spending the rest of my life in Syria, or Lebanon, maybe Jordan; difficult to explain, but there's a powerful ambience in the Middle East that can be compelling to an impressionable, young man—"

Rusty cut him off. "What's 'embreance,' never heard a that before?"

"Ambience is the way one reacts to a specific place and time, how that place and everything in it makes one feel. You could be in a café with friends talking politics or philosophy: you might say the ambience of that place and time was inspiring. Or, you could find yourself with a lover in a room with walls and ceilings of billowing, multicolored silk hangings; a soft, colorful rug on the floor; dozens of sumptuous cushions to lounge upon; perfume-scented breezes; soft lighting. I'd call the ambience of such a place sensual."

Rusty snorted. "Sounds like this fancy whorehouse I went to in Baltimore when I was in the army. Real fancy like, with lotsa cushions and mats spread out on the floor, this pool in the middle, and lotsa flowers an' palms; but with everybody humpin' together on the cushions in the same room, the *embreance* was like a gym and the smell like a locker room."

Jasper grinned. "*Ambiance,* not *embreance*; a man with a poetic gift you are, Mister Samadi. 'Humpin' together on the cushions,' were ya now. You surely know how to turn a phrase, my immense friend."

Rusty didn't like the way the conversation was headed and changed direction. "So, you're not a Muslim?"

"I was brought up Church of England, that's like the Episcopal Church in America."

"You're a Christian, then?"

"Since I was brought up Christian and I never converted to another religion, I guess that makes me a Christian; in name, if nothing else."

Rusty wrinkled his forehead and thought before speaking. "My father and mother was Muslims. When I was little, my father used to read me an' my brother, Ali, from the Muslim bible and we said prayers sometimes. You think that makes me a Muslim?"

Jasper shrugged. "You ever take an oath that you were a Muslim?"

Rusty closed one eye and thought. "What kinda oath?"

"You'd say, 'There is no true God but Allah, and Mohamed is his messenger.'"

"Never done that."

"Not when you said prayers with your father and brother?"

Rusty thought a moment. "No, never."

"Then you're not a Muslim; it's that simple."

Rusty grinned. "That's a good thing, be harder to kill all those people down there if I was one of 'em."

Jasper decided not to pursue the conversation and just nodded.

The doorbell rang, followed by a discreet knock on the door. "That'll be breakfast; hurry, into the bathroom."

For a large man, Rusty moved quickly out of the room.

"One minute," Jasper called, in Farsi. "I'm coming."

* * *

"That was real good." Rusty pushed his chair back from the

table. "I liked that stuff with the eggs, reminds me of Rosa's chili, but different kinda spices. That bread was spicy too, an' really tasty."

"Iranian," Jasper responded. "Iranians make the best bread in the world."

Rusty grinned. "Won't have to worry about GERT no more, or takin' them blue pills neither."

After the breakfast cart was rolled into their suite, Jasper had changed into the two-piece, ihram garment. He retrieved a small plastic case from the breakfast table and walked to the mirror next to the entry door where he unscrewed the caps from the case and placed it and the caps on the mirror table below. "Don't get wound up when I turn around; I'm just putting in new eyes."

Rusty stared, while Jasper, with a practiced hand, tipped back his head and effortlessly inserted a contact lens into each eye, then turned to face Rusty.

"That's amazing!" Rusty exclaimed. "How'd ya do that?"

"Color-tinted contact lenses."

"They can make your eyes change color like that?"

"The lenses are tinted, tinted brown."

Rusty stood, walked toward Jasper, and bent down to examine Jasper's eyes. "You don't look like who you are no more."

Jasper smiled a broad ear-to-ear smile. "That, my brave friend, is because Martin Jasper is about to be consumed by your majestic conflagration. He will perish and I, a brown-eyed, Sudanese peasant, will depart this city leaving old blue-eyed Jasper behind."

"You're goin' back to London?"

"Not a chance; I'm disappearing to an island where the people know me by another name, where they know me well, but have never met Martin Jasper."

Rusty frowned. "Sorry I asked. . . So that's why you're helpin' the Government blow up the Muslim's Ka'aba; so you have the money to go live on your island?"

"Nothing to do with money."

"You really do hate Muslims that much, then?"

Jasper sighed and sat on the edge of the couch. "I don't hate Muslims, I don't hate Jews, or Christians; I don't hate anyone. What we're about here is preserving civilization from the barbarian extremists who've hijacked Islam and would use their distorted version of the religion to tear down millennia of humanist achievement: those who consider women property and relegate them to their ancient position of incomplete men, and second-class humans; who cut off limbs, and gouge out eyes as fit punishment for 'crimes' against religious dogma; those who would replace intellectual freedom with an Orwellian, dictatorship of the mind."

Rusty shook his head. "I don't understand what you're tryin' ta say', is it that we have to blow up their Ka'aba because the Muslims do bad stuff?"

"It's complicated," Jasper replied. "For fifteen-hundred years, until the early seventeenth century, the Catholic Church had a monopoly on religion in Europe. During those fifteen-hundred years, like Islam in the Middle East today, the Church's power extended far beyond religion. In differing forms from place to place, the Church was the government, the police, the lawmaker, and the courts of justice. People who lived in Europe in those days were either Christians or they were infidels. The Church had near absolute authority; break Church laws or threaten the Church authority and an individual became a heretic, and subject to the Church's wrath: excommunication, torture at the hand of the Inquisition, and burning at the stake. The rise of humanism, the Enlightment, the Renaissance, and the Reformation gradually fragmented the powers of the Church and led to a shift of power away from the Church to the nations, the governments. Most people think the constitutional separation of church and state in the West exists to provide us with freedom of religion and protection from persecution. While that's true, more importantly, the separation of church and state also protects us from the domination of religion, any religion."

Rusty laughed. "Martin, sometimes I think you just like to hear yourself talk."

"You might be right." Jasper stood, put his hand on Rusty's shoulder and steered Rusty toward the bedroom. "The device will be here in a few minutes; let's get you ready."

* * *

Although their beards had been trimmed and they were dressed in the pressed white thawbs of Raffles Mecca Palace staff, Rusty recognized the men; they were the driver and the helper from the Mercedes, the men who'd met the bus on the highway and driven Jasper and Rusty to the hotel. The driver was in the process of sliding into a pair of shiny, metallic coveralls. The helper had already donned coveralls, removed his sandals, and was covering his feet with metallic booties. The stainless-steel cart that had been wheeled in earlier with breakfast had been moved to the side, and another, nearly identical cart stood in the center of the room.

The driver zipped up his coveralls and sat on the arm of the couch. "Give us a hand, then," he said to Rusty, holding out two booties. Rusty bent and pulled the metallic booties over the man's feet.

The two, space-suited men donned silvery mittens and stood in front of the cart for Jasper's inspection.

"Excellent!" Jasper said, looking the men over. "Remember, three minutes, not a second more."

The driver nodded. "We could do this in our sleep."

"You go over three minutes' exposure and it'll be a long, long sleep."

Jasper took Rusty's arm and guided him to stand with his back to the doors of the cart. He placed the upper sheet of Rusty's ihram garment over the back of the couch. "You ready?" Jasper asked.

Rusty nodded.

"Remember, just like we rehearsed; out the door and wait by the lift. When you see me approach, push the down button. When you get to the ground floor, go through the lobby and out to the entrance. The driver will be waiting for you; he'll know who you are. Don't forget to—"

"Take off my sandals and put 'em in a plastic bag before I go in the mosque, and step in with my right foot first," Rusty finished the sentence.

"And the ignition switch?"

"I have to push it two times; so if it gets bumped into, it won't go off by accident."

Jasper grinned. "You'll do just fine." He embraced Rusty. "Just fine," he repeated.

Jasper removed his wristwatch and set it on top of the cart. "Your lucky day," he said to the two men. "It's a Rolex, worth about eight-thousand quid." He pointed at the watch. "Push this button as soon as I'm out the door; this hand will come to a stop in exactly three minutes."

Jasper helped the two men pull on their matching silvery hoods, patted Rusty's arm, and opened the door. "Go!" he said, as he stepped through the doorway, and into the hallway.

The helper pressed the button on the Rolex, turned the key that was already in the cart door, and opened the thick, heavy doors. The driver moved Rusty's arms out to the sides and stooped to the open cart doors. In one fluid motion, the two men lifted the bomb out of the cart and onto Rusty's shoulders, and then secured the padded, flesh-colored straps around his torso. While the driver buckled the carbon-fiber fastenings and unscrewed the protective cap from the ignition switch, the helper gathered the ihram from the couch and carefully draped it over Rusty's large body, concealing the bomb.

"Go!" The driver called through his protective hood and opened the door. As Rusty exited and the door closed, the helper pulled off his hood and mitten and pressed the button on the Rolex, while the driver slammed and locked the heavy doors on the cart: "One minute-thirty-eight seconds!" the helper cried. "A new record!"

The driver replaced his silvery mittens with latex gloves, threw another pair to his partner, and took two spray bottles and a bag of cleaning cloths from the bottom of the breakfast cart. He held up two plastic food-storage bags. "Damn! These fingers are still frozen! I'll give 'em a quick microwave. You start in the bedroom and I'll work out here."

"Don't forget to put some prints on the utensils and breakfast dishes," the helper responded.

TWENTY-EIGHT

The bomb was hot against Rusty's bare skin. As he walked toward the elevator, Rusty realized that the bomb was considerably lighter than the mock-up he'd worn and exercised with in Sarasota. *Sneaky,* he thought, *they had me carryin' round a heavier one so the real thing would feel lighter.* With less effort than expected, he strode to the elevator and pushed the down button. Rusty looked back and saw brown-eyed Jasper slowly making his way down the hall toward the bank of elevators.

The middle door opened, the elevator was unoccupied and carried Rusty to the ground floor without stopping. The sumptuous lobby was nearly empty and Rusty moved directly toward the main entrance. Without turning his head he shifted his eyes from side to side to see if anyone was watching. Although he knew Jasper was following, it felt strange to be alone. From the moment they boarded the DSC corporate jet in Florida, until a few minutes ago, Jasper had been Rusty's constant companion: London, Egypt, Sudan; Martin Jasper had never left his side.

* * *

The balding SUV driver was dressed in a baggy, chalk-striped suit and open-necked, white shirt. He smiled, and spoke to Rusty in a language Rusty couldn't understand, and then opened the side door of a bulbous, white Chevy Yukon. Rusty had difficulty climbing into the vehicle. His muscular legs and arms were capable of hauling the additional weight onto the backseat, however, the bulky bomb made it difficult for him to bend. With help from the driver, he folded himself onto the seat. The bulk of the bomb pressing against his abdomen made breathing uncomfortable. He knew the ride to the Grand Mosque would be less than five minutes and pushed into the seat back each time he inhaled. Although the A/C was blowing full blast, Rusty was already sweating.

* * *

Martin Jasper exited from the hotel, crossed the road, and strode purposefully toward the South Gate of the Grand Mosque; the traffic noise and the excited chatter of the pilgrims was deafening. He arrived just as the Chevy Yukon pulled up at the plaza in front of the massive, marble-pillared gates. Towering minarets rose from the walls on either side of the gates. Jasper became one with the homogeneous sea of white ihram garments, and waited patiently while Rusty, with the driver's assistance, extracted himself from the rear seat and walked across the plaza toward the gates.

As he left the SUV Rusty looked at the dashboard clock; it was ten-twenty. He calculated that it had been nearly fifteen minutes since he had been fitted with the bomb; for fifteen minutes he'd been exposed to lethal radiation. Even if he pulled the bomb from his body and let it fall unexploded to the pavement, the radiation had already poisoned his blood and organs and would guarantee a lingering, painful death no matter his course of action. Rusty grinned; from the moment he'd found Tater's broken body he was committed to this day, the day when Allah would no longer be great.

He joined the human river flowing toward the gates and found himself caught up in a group of black African men with tight, curly hair, their deep voices monotonously chanting in an unknown language; their body odor, overwhelming. To his left, Rusty saw a short Asian woman clad in a white nurse's uniform, the crescent moon and star on her headdress replacing the familiar Red Cross. She was consumed with religious fervor, and stared blankly at the gate, tears running down her cheeks. A cluster of men in Arab garb, carrying two small boys, pushed against Rusty's back.

A group of Saudi security guards stood in front of the gate checking the contents of bags and unrolling prayer rugs. As Martin had instructed, Rusty extended his right arm with the rubber ID bracelet issued to Saeed Habibi at Jeddah Airport. The officer in charge scanned the bracelet into a computer; he rose from his seat in front of the monitor, unhurriedly looked Rusty over, and then spoke to the guards operating the metal detector. The guards raised their arms to restrain the other pilgrims from nearing the detector while Rusty nervously passed through. Jasper viewed the security process from twenty feet behind, and when Rusty cleared the metal detector, Jasper was unable to hold back a broad smile; the Caretaker's representative's assistant had been true to his word and had allowed the deadly bomb to enter this sacred place.

Rusty nearly forgot to remove his sandals before entering the mosque and remembered only when he stumbled into one of the African men who'd bent to remove his flip-flops. He awkwardly apologized, pulled off his sandals, and took care to step into the mosque with his right foot.

Inside the mosque, Rusty found himself in an enormous hall, the vast roof suspended several stories above on great marble pillars. To the left, a richly colored, hand-knotted carpet covered what seemed to be an acre of floor where hundreds of pilgrims knelt at prayer. To the right, an aisle flanked by huge marble columns led to an arch, the exit from the hall to the outdoor courtyard and the Ka'aba. Through the archway Rusty indistinctly saw the swarm of white-clad pilgrims circling the Ka'aba; a whirlpool filmed in slow motion.

The pilgrims who'd entered the mosque with Rusty calmly moved to the carpeted section of the hall to pray. Other pilgrims, who'd finished their prayers, rose and walked toward the arch, and the sunlight. Unlike the pilgrims, Rusty skipped the prayers and walked directly down the long aisle towards the outdoors and the sun; it was time to meet his destiny in the courtyard.

As Jasper had taught him, Rusty carefully folded back the ihram sheet over his left shoulder leaving his right shoulder bare. All of the male pilgrims moving toward the courtyard did the same. He checked that the flesh-colored straps over his right shoulder were the only visible component of the bomb harness.

As he stepped through the archway, Rusty was immediately engulfed by waves of pilgrims who'd completed prayers in other halls of the great mosque and were already in the courtyard circling the Ka'aba. He saw that the amorphous mass of humanity he had observed from the hotel window now had separate, individual faces, faces with distinct features and expressions; young and old, dark and fair. For the first time since he'd agreed to carry the bomb, Rusty fully grasped the monstrosity of what he was about to do; these were the faces of innocents he was going destroy, not the face of Mu's killer or of those who'd smashed Tater's head against the wall! In a moment of confusion, he looked over his shoulder and saw that turning back against this pulsing human tide was impossible. He was a dead man, his body poisoned by the deadly radiation invisibly flowing from the demonic fetus perched on his belly; a dead man being carried like flotsam on a white sea of joyous, awestruck pilgrims who, unknowingly, were about to meet their God. He clenched his right hand into a tight fist. "Don't let go, Mu, don't let go," he hoarsely whispered through parched lips.

* * *

Inside the great hall, Martin Jasper maneuvered among the rows of praying pilgrims, and moved to a position on an outside wall, a wall near the courtyard. He lowered himself to his knees, bowed in supplication, then, after touching his forehead to the carpet, straightened and glanced at the miniature GPS device cradled in the palm of his left hand. On the tiny screen, a blue dot that followed Rusty's movements inside the courtyard slowly blinked. At the center of the display was a glowing, fixed white dot, the Ka'aba. When Rusty and his blinking blue light moved within one hundred yards of the Ka'aba, that white dot too would begin to pulse.

* * *

At six-foot-three, Rusty easily saw over the flesh-and-bone ocean of ihram white to the Ka'aba; it was several stories high, much larger than it had appeared from the hotel window, and was covered in black cloth, trimmed near the top with an ornate gold border.

The entire courtyard was heaving with human bodies while more, and still more, pilgrims continued to thrust their way in from the dozens of gates spaced along the perimeter of the Grand Mosque. Those pilgrims on the outer edges of the rotating whirlpool moved at a faster pace than those closer to the Ka'aba. Jasper had explained this was a part of the ritual of the tawaf, the circumnavigation of the Ka'aba; pilgrims moved quickly for the first few of the required seven counter-rotations, and then, slowed for the remaining three or four. The pilgrims were chanting prayers in a multitude of languages; some softly, others shrilly crying out, caught up in an ecstasy of religious passion.

Rusty was profusely sweating; salty rivulets flowed from his scalp into his eyes and onto his bare, right shoulder, then ran under his ihram sheet, and collected along the edges of the harness and the bomb. With so many thousands of people pressed together, pilgrims constantly bumped and pushed against one another. An old man with a long white beard shoved an elbow into Rusty's right side. Instinctively, Rusty pushed back with his forearm, forcing the man to stumble backward into a group of dark-skinned women, scattering them like bowling pins onto the marble courtyard floor. Rusty didn't notice the old man or the women; he was transfixed, his gaze fixed on the Ka'aba; as if in a hypnotic trance, he pressed onward. Jasper's instructions were for Rusty to move to the center of the circling throng as quickly as possible, and then, during the middle of the first rotation, to weave his way toward the Ka'aba where he would detonate the bomb.

The unfamiliar invasion of strangers continually pressing against his torso, arms and legs, the overwhelming din of the prayers and chants, the heat of the sun, the overpowering body odor, the weight of the bomb and the chafing of the harness against his skin, all spurred Rusty to move more quickly toward the Ka'aba than Jasper had instructed. A woman behind him stumbled and jammed her toenail into his bare heal, painfully tearing away a small chunk of flesh. His senses were being overwhelmed and he was rapidly losing control of his emotions. Rusty violently shook his head; panicked by the claustrophobic nightmare that engulfed him, he began to aggressively push pilgrims out of his path. Some glared at him, others, seeing his large body and wild expression quickly moved out of the way.

Sweat continued to stream into his burning eyes, it was becoming increasingly difficult for him to see, and the faces surrounding him were now indistinguishable from one another. Suddenly, the bomb felt disturbingly hot, fiery hot against his skin; the heat and weight of the bomb was sucking out the last of his energy.

Rusty was wheezing and breathing heavily; he found it difficult to move his legs. He started to feel lightheaded and disoriented and knew he was nearing physical and emotional collapse. Then, only a dozen yards ahead, on a corner of the Ka'aba, he saw the black stone in its silver mount. He pulled together the remnants of his physical strength and plunged into the knot of pilgrims who were swarming like locusts around the black stone, jostling each other and competing for a place where they could stand to touch or kiss the stone's ancient surface.

Rusty turned his face toward the sky. "Hold on to me, Mu, don't let go," Rusty shouted. He thrust his right hand under the sweat-soaked ihram sheet searching for the bomb's ignition switch. His trembling fingers surrounded the lethal button, but he hesitated. He felt Mu's soft hand under his fingers, covering the bomb's ignition switch. Rusty's rapidly failing mind struggled to understand Mu's intent; was she trying to help him ignite the bomb, or was she shielding the button from his touch? It was Rusty's last conscious thought—an excruciating, sting rocketed through the muscles and nerves of his left arm, shot to his thick neck and then rushed to his chest. His heart spasmed then stalled, and his great body violently trembled. He was conscious, but paralyzed, completely immobile, rooted like a tree before the Ka'aba. Rusty's stricken heart stopped beating. His body violently shook as if in an epileptic seizure. The nerve cells in his oxygen-starved brain started chaotically firing, burning his organs, flesh and skin in an electric collage of agony.

The clamor of the pilgrims in the courtyard ceased and Rusty's world grew silent. His eyesight shut down, and the great hulk of the Ka'aba before him became an indistinct shadow. Vertigo overcame his last sensory connection with the world and Rusty fell hard, his left side crashing against the unyielding marble tiles, his head bouncing like an unripe melon. His quivering fingers still surrounded the ignition switch; his large hand trembled under the sodden white sheet, trembled, and then fell still.

The Saudi security guards standing at either side of the black stone saw the disruption around Rusty's fallen body. One stepped down from his perch and began to move in Rusty's direction.

* * *

Martin Jasper ended his "prayers," stood, and bowed his head. On the screen of the tiny GPS device concealed in the palm of Jasper's hand, the white dot that represented the Ka'aba was now rapidly pulsing; signaling that Rusty was in range of the target, well within a hundred yards. Jasper began to grin, but then, to his horror, he realized that the blue dot on the screen, Rusty's blue dot, was no longer blinking; Rusty had stopped moving. Something had gone terribly wrong. Jasper bit his lip, inhaled through his nose then forcefully exhaled. With his thumb, he slid open what appeared to be a battery cover on the back of the hand-held device, exposing a miniature toggle switch. "Poor sods," Jasper muttered under his breath as he flipped the switch, opening the gates of Hell and turning the courtyard into a poisonous inferno.

TWENTY-NINE

Wednesday 5:10 AM EST, Cable News Network
"Middle East sources are reporting an explosion at the Masjid al Haram Mosque, also called the Grand Mosque, in Mecca, Saudi Arabia. The Saudi Government has closed its borders, grounded all flights into or out of the Kingdom, and cut off telephone and Internet traffic. The explosion reportedly occurred during the Hajj, the annual pilgrimage of millions of Muslims from all over the world to the Holy Cities of Mecca and Medina. The Grand Mosque is the holiest place in Islam, the direction Muslims face when they pray."

Wednesday 5:35 AM EST, Cable News Network
"We're receiving more information on the explosion at the Grand Mosque in Mecca, Saudi Arabia, reported earlier. Satellite imagery has confirmed an incident at the Masjid al Haram Mosque; images indicate considerable damage to the Grand Mosque, and apparently, the destruction of the Ka'aba, or House of God, an ancient, holy structure within the Grand Mosque that Muslims face when they pray from anywhere in the world. This apparent attack occurred during the Hajj, the annual pilgrimage of millions to Mecca and the Grand Mosque, and so it's probable, but unconfirmed, that the death toll from the explosion could be extensive. So far, the Saudi Government has not issued a statement. All communication links into and out of the Kingdom continue to be shut down. With background on the Grand Mosque, the Ka'aba, and the Hajj pilgrimage, we turn to Doctor Ashrem al Haqul from the Department of Middle East Studies at George Washington University; Doctor al Haqul—"

Wednesday 6:00 AM EST, Cable News Network
"This amateur video was taken by a Hajj pilgrim in the aftermath

of the powerful explosion earlier this morning at the Grand Mosque in Mecca, Saudi Arabia. The explosion, now believed to be a terrorist attack, occurred at approximately four AM Eastern time, that's eleven AM in Mecca. It clearly shows hundreds of dead and wounded Hajj pilgrims thrown together in the courtyard of the Mosque, where they were taking part in the ritual circumnavigation of the Ka'aba. The Ka'aba, or House of God, the most sacred structure in Islam, can be seen to have been extensively damaged, nearly destroyed. Communications channels and air traffic into and out of Saudi Arabia remain closed; this video clip was transmitted before communications shut down. The annual Hajj attracts more than three million Muslim pilgrims each year. Muslim families around the globe are anxiously awaiting news of their relatives and loved ones taking part in this year's pilgrimage. The following video from the two-thousand-ten Hajj shows pilgrims in the courtyard completing the tawaf, the seven-time ritual circumnavigation of the Ka'aba."

Wednesday 10:00 AM EST, A Statement from the Government of Saudi Arabia — All Broadcast and Cable Networks
His Excellency—the Representative of the Islamic Kingdom of Saudi Arabia to the United States of America
"This morning in the Holy City of Mecca, in the Islamic Kingdom of Saudi Arabia, there was a vicious attack upon the Mosque of the Noble Prophet, peace be upon him, and the pilgrims of Allah's Inviolable House. A suicide bomber, posing as a pilgrim, detonated a sophisticated, lethal explosive device in the Masjid al Haram, known in the West as the Grand Mosque; this attack was carried out while a multitude of pilgrims were gathered there at the beginning of their sacred Hajj or Umrah journey. The bomb was a Radiological Dispersal Device, a dirty bomb. The force of the explosion immediately took the lives of hundreds of pilgrims; injuries are estimated to be over a thousand. The radioactive materials dispersed by the bomb, over time, will kill and sicken

many others and may render the area where the device exploded inaccessible to humans for some extended period of time. Radiological danger is limited to the relatively small, specific area where the device was detonated; this was not an atomic or nuclear explosion and poses no immediate radiation danger to the residents of Mecca, Saudi Arabia, or any other country.

"Mecca has excellent hospitals and medical facilities to care for local residents and pilgrims. However, there is limited capability to treat radiological poisoning. Since the Holy City of Mecca can be entered only by Muslims, the Kingdom has formally requested specialist medical assistance from the countries of the Arab League and countries with significant Muslim populations.

"In two hours' time, seven PM in Mecca and twelve noon Eastern in the United States, telephone and Internet service into and out of the Kingdom will be restored. However, connection time will be restricted to five minutes. By tomorrow morning, an Internet site will begin to post the names of the dead and the injured. Access information for that site will be distributed to media outlets worldwide. Additional statements will be forthcoming as more details emerge."

Thursday 11:00 AM EST, Cable News Network

"A news conference with Saudi Arabian Security Forces is underway and currently being broadcast on Saudi Television and Al Jazeera, the Arabic language news network. Earlier in the conference, a Saudi spokesman disclosed the identity of those allegedly responsible for yesterday's terrorist bombing of the Grand Mosque in Mecca. Authorities claim they have convincing evidence that two Iranians, Heydar Ganji and his cousin Saeed Habibi, carried out the suicide bombing. Ganji is the son, and Habibi the nephew of Mohsen Ganji, a wealthy Iranian manufacturer who is closely connected with Iran's religious leaders. Officials claim the two men stayed at a five-star hotel directly across from the Grand Mosque where a shielded cart with high levels of residual radiation, and bearing both men's fingerprints, was discovered in the suite they occupied for two days. It's believed the cart was used to transport the radioactive bomb from its place of assembly to the hotel suite. Further, a dummy bomb and shoulder harness with fingerprints belonging to Habibi were discovered in a bedroom closet. Saudi authorities have conjectured that Habibi, a tall man, wore the dummy bomb under his robe to pass as someone with a large belly, so that when he put on the real bomb, he wouldn't draw attention from the hotel staff. Management and staff at the hotel have identified photos from Hajj identification papers as Ganji and Habibi.

"Confirmed deaths from the bombing posted on the Saudi Security Forces website now exceed twelve hundred. In conformance with Muslim religious practices forbidding cremation or embalming of the dead, victims are being interred in mass graves in the desert outside the City of Mecca."

Thursday 7:00 PM EST, Fox News

"Usually reliable sources in Caracas, Venezuela, have disclosed to Fox News the origin of the deadly radioisotopes used in the powerful dirty bomb that was detonated yesterday at the Grand Mosque in Mecca, Saudi Arabia. These sources claim that the deadly radioisotopes originated in the Islamic Republic of Iran and were transported sometime last spring by a Lebanese Hezbollah agent from Tehran to Caracas by Conviasa, the National Airline of Venezuela, on an unscheduled flight. These same sources have produced shipping documents, they say support their claim."

The New York Times

"In an unprecedented action today, the Arab League, the notoriously fractious regional organization of twenty-two Arab States, voted to condemn Iran for sponsoring the terrorist bombing of the Masjid al Haram, the Grand Mosque in Mecca, two weeks ago. This action was clearly meant to preempt the United Nations Security Council session next week that will address Iran's culpability in the attack on the Grand Mosque, and to assert the Arab League's hegemony in matters specific to Islam in the Middle East and North Africa.

"The League's unexpected and unambiguous condemnation of Iran follows last week's raid on the Tri-Gen Medical Technology Company in Nabatieh, a predominantly Shia area, in southern Lebanon. Evidence obtained during the raid unmistakably established Tri-Gen as the builder of the Grand Mosque bomb. Documents, shielded shipping containers, and information obtained during the interrogation of Tri-Gen's chief engineer support earlier reports from Venezuela that implicate Iran as the source of the bomb's deadly radioisotope components. The registered owners of Tri-Gen include an Iranian expat currently residing in Lebanon, as well as Mohsen Ganji, the father and uncle of the two Iranian suicide bombers."

BBC World Service, Radio News

"Violent demonstrations condemning Iran for sponsoring the terrorist bombing of the Grand Mosque in Mecca continue to spread throughout the Islamic world. Most recently, in Jakarta, the capital of Indonesia, an angry mob estimated at over a thousand, threw firebombs at the Embassy of the Islamic Republic of Iran, chanting slogans usually reserved for the United States and the West, and demanding retribution for the destruction of the Holy Ka'aba. Reports from the site indicate police were doing little to restrain the crowds. Tens of thousands of Indonesian migrant workers are employed in Iran as housemaids and menials. Indonesian officials report 174 Indonesian pilgrims among the known Hajj casualties.

"Deaths from the dirty bomb detonated at the Masjid al Haram Mosque currently stand at 3,104. Saudi officials state that more than a thousand additional fatalities are expected as more Hajj pilgrims, and medical workers who rushed to aid the victims, continue to succumb to the delayed effects of deadly radiation poisoning.

"Efforts to assess the extent of radiation contamination at the Mosque have been constrained by the prohibition forbidding non-Muslims from entering the City of Mecca. After visiting the Mosque earlier this week, a team of Muslim Environmental Engineers, recruited from Europe and the UK estimated that it would take five years or more for the courtyard and much of the Mosque to be safe for human use. Robin Johor, the British spokesman for the engineering team summed up the situation: 'There's not much anyone can do. Tearing down most of the Mosque, removing thousands of tons of earth from the courtyard, and carting all that radioactive material off into the desert isn't a realistic alternative. We'll just have to wait for the Strontium-90 and Cesium-137 to decay to nonlethal levels. That'll take some time.'"

EPILOGUE

"You finally shook the flu?"

"Took nearly a month," the Secretary responded. "Either it was an unusually powerful strain this year, or my immune capabilities are wearing thin."

"If I were you, I'd go with the strong strain theory," General Thornton replied. "No sense giving comfort to your enemies."

The Secretary grinned. "You think I have enemies?"

"A few less today than you did last week."

The Secretary maintained the grin. "The Saudi Air Force performed real well, better than I'd expected; a tribute to your guys in Idaho who trained 'em."

"Iowa—the Saudi pilots learned to fly their F-15s in Iowa. The very best of them fly out of the Prince Sultan Airbase. They're the squads who took out the Revolutionary Guard HQ buildings in Tehran and killed the—"

"The Supreme Leader, the Ayatollah?"

Fidel nodded. "That's what I been told, same guys. What surprised me the most was the Egyptians; they must have put near a hundred F-16s in the sky; I'm told the UAE did a hell of a job interrupting command and control, and even the Kuwaiti Air Force and their F-18s were remarkably effective in air-to-air. I mean, we knew the Iranian Air Force was flying some obsolete stuff, but I guess their newer Russian, Chinese, and homemade aircraft didn't make up the difference. Think you can get me a peek at the intelligence reports? I'm absolutely astounded that Iran's air-defense systems failed so quickly."

The Secretary tapped his pen on the desktop. "See what I can do; perhaps the Sunnis had a little help from their friends? You're asking for some pretty sensitive material, but I'll see what I can do."

Fidel nodded. "The administration doesn't intend to get

involved in this war?"

"Not our war, you and Nick saw to that. We'll have to patrol the edges of course; make sure the Russians or Chinese don't meddle, keep the Israelis from shooting themselves in the foot."

The Secretary pushed back into his chair. "Turning to another matter—you've finalized arrangements with Taylor Donner?"

General Thornton nodded. "Taylor's in; his only concern was making sure DSC would remain at arm's length. He's decided on how to do that."

"Oh?"

"Taylor's gonna move up to Chairman and replace himself at CEO. He offered the job to his sister's husband Rick Cappa but he turned it down; you know Rick?"

The Secretary smiled. "Just about everyone on the hill knows Rick; solid guy."

"Taylor's got an internal candidate and is about to make an offer."

"When's this gonna happen?"

"Taylor didn't say, soon, I hope."

"Why soon?"

"There's a time-sensitive opportunity. You know much about Buddhism?"

The Secretary cocked his head. "Buddhism? Not really."

"Ever hear of the Panchen Lama, the Chinese Lama?"

"No, but I guess you're gonna tell me," the Secretary replied.

"About fifteen years ago, when the Chinese invaded Tibet, they kidnapped the appointed Panchen Lama, the second highest in the Tibetan Buddhist leadership hierarchy; he was only five or six years old at the time. They took him and his entire family to Beijing. Next, the Chinese replaced the young Panchen Lama with a child they'd selected. People in Tibet derisively call the replacement the 'Chinese Lama.' Upset a lot of folks. The Dalai Lama is the Tibetan Buddhist head of state in exile; he's the Buddhist spiritual leader and is supposed to choose the Panchen

Lama, not the Communist Party. Since this usurpation, the 'Chinese Lama' has been a stooge for the Communist leadership and supported their repressive policies in Tibet."

"Not a formula for winning Tibetan's hearts and minds, I suspect? But isn't this just a local issue?"

"There's more," General Thornton replied. "The current Dali Lama is in his late seventies. After the Chinese put down the Tibetan uprising in nineteen-fifty-nine, the Dali Lama fled to India and exile. He won the Nobel Peace Prize in nineteen-eighty-nine, is a respected world figure, and an unceasing voice for freeing Tibet from Chinese rule. Naturally, when he dies, the Communist Party would like to replace the Dali Lama with someone more sympathetic to their propaganda."

"Like the Panchen Lama?"

Fidel grinned. "Yeah, but there's a problem with that. A new Dali Lama is considered the reincarnation of the previous Dali Lama. After the Dali Lama's death, a 'committee' of the Tibetan Buddhist hierarchy will search among the male population for the reincarnation of the Dali Lama in the form of a young boy; when they find the reincarnation, that boy becomes the new Dali Lama. The Communist Party would have a difficult time selling their reincarnated pick for Dali Lama to the Tibetans. Because of his age, the Panchen Lama can't be a reincarnation, he's not a candidate. But, and here's the important part, as number two, the Panchen Lama has considerable influence over who is selected."

"Go on."

"Recently there have been reports that the original Panchen Lama is alive and living outside of Beijing; he'd be about twenty-two now. These persistent rumors, along with a clumsy, attempted power grab by the current Panchen Lama, and, the fact that he's universally despised throughout Tibet as a Chinese toady, are making the Chinese very nervous. Tibet's never really been integrated into China, and the last thing the Chinese need is for the world to watch another severe repression, another

Tiananmen Square, on the nightly news."

The Secretary nodded. "Okay, I see where you're going; an opportunity for a bit of mischief in Tibet at the expense of the Chinese Communists?"

General Thornton leaned back in his chair and grinned. "Exactly."

At Roundfire we publish great stories. We lean towards the spiritual and thought-provoking. But whether it's literary or popular, a gentle tale or a pulsating thriller, the connecting theme in all Roundfire fiction titles is that once you pick them up you won't want to put them down.